PENGUIN

BOOK OF S

JACK KEROUAC was born in Lowell, Massachusetts, in 1922, the youngest of three children in a Franco-American family. He attended local Catholic and public schools and won a scholarship to Columbia University in New York City, where he met Allen Ginsberg and William S. Burroughs. His first novel, *The Town and the City,* appeared in 1950, but it was *On the Road,* first published in 1957, that made Kerouac one of the best-known writers of his time. Publication of his many other books followed, among them *The Subterraneans, Big Sur,* and *The Dharma Bums.* Kerouac's books of poetry include *Mexico City Blues, Scattered Poems, Pomes All Sizes, Heaven and Other Poems, Book of Blues,* and *Book of Haikus.* Kerouac died in St. Petersburg, Florida, in 1969, at the age of forty-seven.

GEORGE CONDO is a painter and sculptor who has exhibited extensively in both the United States and Europe, with works in the collections of the Whitney Museum of American Art, The Museum of Modern Art, New York, and many other institutions. In 1999, Condo received an Academy Award from the American Academy of Arts and Letters and in 2005 he received the Francis J. Greenberger Award. He is represented by Luhring Augustine in New York, Andrea Caratsch Galley in Zurich, and Sprüth Magers Lee in London.

ALSO BY JACK KEROUAC

JACK KEROUAC

BOOK OF SKETCHES

· 1952–57 ·

Introduction by
GEORGE CONDO

PENGUIN POETS

PENGUIN BOOKS

Published by the Penguin Group

Penguin Group (USA) Inc., 375 Hudson Street, New York, New York 10014, U.S.A.

Penguin Group (Canada), 90 Eglinton Avenue East, Suite 700, Toronto, Ontario,
Canada M4P 2Y3
(a division of Pearson Penguin Canada Inc.)

Penguin Books Ltd, 80 Strand, London WC2R 0RL, England

Penguin Ireland, 25 St Stephen's Green, Dublin 2, Ireland (a division of Penguin Books Ltd)

Penguin Group (Australia), 250 Camberwell Road, Camberwell, Victoria 3124, Australia
(a division of Pearson Australia Group Pty Ltd)

Penguin Books India Pvt Ltd, 11 Community Centre, Panchsheel Park,
New Delhi–110 017, India

Penguin Group (NZ), cnr Airborne and Rosedale Roads, Albany, Auckland 1310,
New Zealand (a division of Pearson New Zealand Ltd)

Penguin Books (South Africa) (Pty) Ltd, 24 Sturdee Avenue, Rosebank,
Johannesburg 2196, South Africa

Penguin Books Ltd, Registered Offices: 80 Strand, London WC2R 0RL, England

First published in Penguin Books 2006

1 3 5 7 9 10 8 6 4 2

LIBRARY OF CONGRESS CATALOGING-IN-PUBLICATION DATA
Kerouac, Jack, 1922–1969.
Book of sketches, 1952–53 / Jack Kerouac ; introduction by George Condo.
p. cm.
ISBN 0-14-200215-1
1. Kerouac, Jack, 1922–1969—Notebooks, sketchbooks, etc. I. Title.
PS3521.E735B667 2006
818'.5403—dc22   2005044535

Printed in the United States of America
Set in Sabon with AT Sackers Gothic
Designed by Victoria Hartman

Book of Sketches

Jack Kerouac

(Proving that sketches
aint Verse

But Only What Is

o o o o o o

Dedicated to the memory of

Caroline Kerouac Blake

INTRODUCTION

Thoughts about Jack Kerouac

Read this *Book of Sketches* and you'll be amazed at what a genius Jack Kerouac was.

These poems just breathe and flow, and when Jack plays the Blues, which he often does, his blues are truly sad—they are sadness without humor, without the joking and backslapping that come from good times. They are the real unfunny truth. Like when his older brother Gerard died. This is one of the saddest poems ever written.

I learned a lot from Jack, and I can say all this not being a writer. At the age of fourteen he was the first radical I ever heard of. When I first became aware that he wrote his novel *The Subterraneans* in one long stretch, unrevised straight out of his head in three days, and that he had a "steel trap" memory—it was the combination of these two very important factors that inspired a new way of painting for me. From then on I combined memory, speed, and spontaneity to create most of my work. I relied on the Kerouacian notion of "the unrevised method of creation," and it became the key to a pure uncontrollable mastery of chaos.

As a reader, you would think Kerouac was talking, not writing. Yet it was precisely everyday speech that he was able to conjure up. He, like Jackson Pollock, found a way to take something all of us see and use every day and turn it into Art. This new language of Jack Kerouac was the one we had always been speaking. You just had to know what you were talking about before you spoke.

Jack's concept of writing was also very art-inspired—he drew on André Masson's Automatic Painting and Charlie Parker's informed improvisations to carve out his unique style and destination. He called upon Leonardo da Vinci's method of observation in his studies of flowers, storms, anatomy, and physiognomy. Jack is to literature what Charlie Parker was to music or Jackson Pollock was to painting. It's that simple. Proust should be invoked here, too. He must have been one of Kerouac's favorite writers because he used him to describe Miles Davis's phrasing in order to enhance a cultural value that had not yet been perceived—he spoke of Miles's playing "eloquent phrases, just like Marcel Proust."

To look at Edward Hopper's paintings of the late 1920s and early 1930s is to see the destitute ambience of New York City and its existential paradox—it is a place at once industrious and at the same time empty, lonely, and unanswered. These qualities are found in some of Kerouac's poetical sketches—gas stations, old barges, oil tankers, silhouettes of a positive industry set against dark empty exteriors that have been forgotten and misplaced:

Indian land or an old gold mine, towns at one time prosperous now distinctly gone, reflecting an America that no one wanted to admit was still there.

Jack himself had a cubist take on Hopper—not unlike Joseph Stella's faceted Brooklyn Bridge—cubist in the sense that the fragmentation is not of imagery but of time and space. The elements of chronology in these sketches are here of no importance. In fact, Jack has made a note, "Not Necessarily Chronological," this being on his mind—in a larger sense referring to all the poems in the *Book of Sketches*, but also referring to the sequence of words within each poem. That's what gives a "sketch" its edge, the fractured, almost "cut-up" feel that the descriptions carry. They seem to be running straight at you and then split up unexpectedly into multiple directions simultaneously, ending on a resolved note somehow related and yet striking out in a new direction.

Unlike Hopper, though, Kerouac did not long for the past—he did not reminisce for the sake of nostalgia—or transpose the European masters' sensibility. Rather, in the 1950s he broke free and prophetically dreamed a future world of young people wearing Levi's and being cut loose from all the crumbling conventions. Jack saw into the future, he lived in the future. That is exactly what happened in the 1960s to society, but by then Jack was too old and self-abused to have any pleasure from the world he predicted.

As the sketches tell us, anything that Jack saw was

important. Anything that caught his eye and that he wrote about became priceless. Because in the way that an artist like Picasso could see with his brush, Jack could see with his pen. He was able to capture the spirit of his time without making anything up. And as it came to us from nowhere it certainly was astounding how concrete it all is now. It is as if the only true picture of humanity we will ever have was given to us by Jack Kerouac. All else is false and dressed up. Only Jack and Vincent van Gogh told the inner truth.

—*George Condo, November 2005*

BOOK OF SKETCHES

JACK KEROUAC

Printed Exactly As They Were Written
On the Little Pages in the Notebooks
I Carried in My Breast Pocket 1952
Summer to 1954 December............

(Not Necessarily Chronological)

FIRST BOOK

Rocky Mt Aug. 7 '52

Changed now to
dungaree shorts, gaudy
green sandals, blue vest
with white borders & a
little festive lovergirl ribbon
in her hair Carolyn prepares
the supper—
  "I better go over there &
fix that lawnmower," says
Paul standing in the kitchen
with LP at his thigh.
  "Supper'll be ready at
six."
  Glancing at his watch
Paul goes off - to his landlord
Jack up the road—a man his
age, of inherited wealth,
who spends all day in big
Easonburg walking around
or sitting in his vast brick
house (Jacky Lee's father)

or walking down the road
to see his 2 new cows—

On the kitchen floor is
a pan of dog meal mixed
with milk & water but the
bird dog Bob isnt hungry,
just let out of the pen
he lays greedily sopping
up happy in-house hours
under the d.r. table — a
big affectionate dopey
beauty with great bony
snakehead & big brown eyes
& heartshaped mottled
ears falling like the locks
of a pretty girl do fall —
in the Fall a gliding phantom
in the pale fields.
  Carolyn takes a pile
of dishes from the cupboard
& silverware from the
drawer & carries them

into the diningroom. Out of
the ref. she takes ready
to bake biscuit doughs &
unwraps them from their
cellophane, stuffs waste paper
in the corner bag that
sits in a wastebasket

out of sight — She
prepares the aluminum
silex for coffee — never
puts an extra scoop for
the pot — makes weak
American housewife coffee
— but who's to
notice, the Prez. of the
Waldorf Astoria? — She
slams a frying pan on a
burner — singing "I hadnt
anyone till you & with
my lonely heart demanding
it, f-a-i-t-h must
have a hand in it — "

mistaking "fate" — Out
comes the bacon & the
yellow plastic
basket of eggs — What's
she going to make? Under
the faucet she cleans
garden fresh tomatos
from Mrs Harris' —
  She's boiling potatos in a
pot — they've been there a
half hour — Thru her
little kitchen cupboard

window, framed like a
picture, see the old
redroofed flu cure barn
of the X farm — weary
gray wood in the eternities
of time — rickety poles
around it — the tobacco,
already picked from
the bottom a foot up,
pale & fieldsy before the
solemn backdrop of
that forest bush —
One intervening sad English
cone haystack — The
little children of the
Carolina suppertimes see
this & think: "And does
the forest need to eat?
In the night that's
coming does the forest
know? Why is that dish
cloth hanging there so
still — & like the
forest — has no name
I know of — gloop — "
Carolyn Blake is making
bacon & eggs & boiled
potatos for supper because

lately the family's been
eating up breakfast
foods — just cereal & toast —

"Hm what pretty bacon,"
she says out loud. On
the radio now's the
Lone Ranger. Lingering
statics clip & clop
amongst its William
Tell Overtures — a
rooster foolish crows —
  Hand on hip, feet
crossed, casually, a cig
burning out in the ashtray,
she picks the bacon over
with a long cook fork.
"Hum hum hum" she hums.

  Paul, having fixed the Jack
lawn mower, is in the yard
  finishing the part of the lawn
last overlooked. The
deep rich fat grass lies in
serried heaps along the
trail of his machine
with the ditch, the road,
& the white road sign

"Easonburg" & yellow
"Stop" sign beyond — &
signs on a post pointing in
all the directions ←
Route 95   2 → US 64
↓ Rocky Mt 3 ↑ Sandy
Cross 4 — Paul, hat off,
sleeves rolled, glumly &
absentmindedly pushes at
his work; the motor makes
a drowsy suppertime growl
like the sound of a motor-
boat on some mystic lake
— At the crossroads store
groups of farmers have
gathered & smoke & sit
now. Heavenly mystical
lights have meanwhile
appeared in the sky as
the great machinery
continues in the High.

Intense interest is being
shown in the lawncutter —
Jack himself has just driven
over (on his way to town)
& is parked on lawn's edge
discussing it with a young

farmer in overalls & white &
green baseball cap who app.
w. to buy it—Little
Paul runs to hear them
talk—At the store
five people are watching
intently. Men are be-
mused by machines. Am-
ericans, by new, efficient
machines; Jack had the
money to buy a deluxe
cutter—2 Negros
& 2 white farmers stare
intently at Paul in his
lawn, from the store, as
he backs up the car
to get to the grass
underneath it—Not once
has he lookt up & acknowledged
his watchers—works on.
Jack has driven off proudly
—Still another man
joins the watchers—&
now even George steps
out to see—now that
Jack's driven off to whom
he hasnt spoken in years—
his twin brother. In Southern

accents — "Thats whut
<u>ah</u> think!" — they
discuss that splendid
grasscutter — Cars come
& park, & go — Cars
hurry on the hiway to
home,
  "Wait till after
supper," says Carolyn to
LP, "we're ready to
eat now — " as
  he complains
    "Ah — nao!"

but the complaint's not
serious & doesnt last
long — And the air
is fragrant from cut
grass. "Come eat!"
  And suddenly not a
soul's at the store as
for other & similar &
just as blank rea-
sons, they've gone to
  the silence
  the suppers of their own
   mystery.

Why should a chair be far
from a book case!
 P: "Well that confound
      yard is mowed."
C: "Fi-na-<u>lee</u>."
 P: "Eat some supper
      boy."
C: — "What is it 27
     now? 28? It musta
     gone up, I thought
     it was 26."
 P: (eating) (to LP) Eat
     yr. beans, boy.
     Better eat up chabeans, —
     boy.

But all was not
always so peaceful with
the Blakes

When LP was born & lay
like a little turd in a
rich white basket in the
hospital (& the Grandma
& Uncle of his future peered
at him thru the slot in
the maternity door — &
the young nurse with glup-

cloth on her mouth making
smiling eyes — & the
little mother half dead
in her bed. A premature
birth, he weighed 2 lbs.,
like so many links of
sausage or one modest
bologna; the ordeal cost
Paul $1,000 — which he
didnt have — Only a
miracle saved Mother &
Son anyway. The young
doctor said sententiously
"Long before Christ
there was a Greek who
found out why mothers
die from shock — "
he emphasized "<u>long be-
fore</u> Christ" in this natty
million dollar Duke Medical
Center where the only hint
of Christ lay if any in
the English-style minis-
ters' dormitory (students
for the ministry played
pingpong with their fiancees
in a fresh painted base-
ment, the emptiness of

modern Southern & American
life) — "<u>long before Christ</u>"
said the young doctor — as
Carolyn lay in a coma
in the quiet shade drawn
room — & the presence
of his Meek & Sorrowful
Humility hung like
molasses with air —

That was when Paul was
being sent from one town
to the other by the Tel Co
& never had enough money
for all he wanted, they
had a house on the
other side of RM, making
payments at a debilitating
rate of interest that
would eventually force
the house from them —
Paul a veteran of Palau
& Okinawa, an infantry
man of the island jungles,
now being usured & screwed
by nonJew Southern realtors
with bibles on their mantle
shelves & respectable

white shirts — sure, sure, —
 the dark rain splattered
 on the lonely house as
he waited nights for C
 & the baby to come home —
"She can never have another
child — " & across the
road from the
house, in the thicket
woods, rain, rain of the South
washed the sorrow & the
deep & something mourned
— & something whisp-
ered to Paul: "You were
born in the woods — your
father was a farmer —
son of these rains — this
wilderness — wretched
victim of usurers &
 bitter pain — yr. wife
 has had yr. heir — you
 sit alone in night —
 dont let yr face hang,
 dont let yr arms fall —
 Doom is yr name —
 Paul Death is yr name —

Paul Nothingness in the
big wild, wide & empty
world that hates you
is your name — Sit
here glooming all you
want — in debt, dark,
sad — Alone — You'll
lose this house, you'll lose
the 5, 6 dollars in yr
pocket — you'll lose the
car in the yard — you'll
lose the yard — you've
gained a wife & child —
almost lost them? They'll
be lost eventually — a
grave that sinks from
the foot, that telegraphs
in dirt the sinking of a
manly chest — awaits
   thee — and they — &
thou art an animal
dying in the wilderness —
Groo, groo, poor man
— groo — only the
heavens & the arcs
will ac-cept thee —
& Knowledge of heaven
& the arcs is not for

thee — so die, die,
die — & be silent —
Paul Blake in the
night, Paul Blake
in the No Carolina
rainy night . . ."
  It took years to make
up the death; C. came
back feeble, pale, nervous;
took nervous pains with
the frail & tiny child;

the months rolled — one
of the bird dogs died of
the St Vitus dance —
in the mud — Only
old Bob survived, sitting
in wait for his master
at gray dusks — The
Autumn came, the winter
laid a carpet of one
inch snow, the Spring
made pines smell sweet
& powerful, the summer
sent his big haze-heat
to burn a hole thru
clouds & swill
up steams from fecund

earth — lost earth —
The Co. transferred
Paul from town to
town — Kinston — Tar
boro — Henderson
— (home of his folks) —
back to Kinston —
Rocky Mt. — Little
Paul grew — & cried
— & learned to suffer —
& cried — & learned
to laugh — & cried —
& learned to be still —
& suffered — Groo, groo,
the heavens dont care —
It had not always
been so easy & calm
as now at suppertime,
in BE, 1952 —
Hateful bitch of a
world, it wouldnt
ever last.

Yes, Yes, there they are
the poor sad people
of the South on Sat-
urday afternoon at
the Crossroads store —

Not so sad as heaven
watching but all the
more lost—all the
more lost—That
poor fat Negro woman
with her festive straw
hat for a joke but has
to be assisted from the
store where she super-
vised the week's grocery
purchases—on her
  crutches; and old
Albino Freckles her
  gaunt ghostly farmer
  husband, comes tott-
ering after on his cane
—& they are deposited
in the car, nephew Jim
slowly wheels the old
family Buick (1937)
from the store—groceries
safe in the old boot trunk,
another week's food
sustenance for the clan
in its solitudes of
corn—
    Sat Afternoon in
the South—the

Jesus singers are al-
ready hot for come-
Sunday tomorrow on
that radio — "Jee-
zas — " 4, Five cars
are parked on one
side alone of that
store — & a truck —

and a bicycle — The
purchases are going
strong — inside rumbling
business, George cigar-in-
mouth is storing up his
Midas profits — only
the other day he fired
Clarence for being
late after seeing his
father at the hospital,
after five times driving
 his useless bucktooth
wife to & fro the hospital
— out there's sadness
enough without having
to run into that —
 Here comes a flat
wagon, mule drawn,
with fat Pop, son &

granddotter, black,
all sitting legs adangle,
they didnt want to
shop his prices at George,
coming from another
down-the-road store —
eating the bought tidbits
of Saturday, — poverty,
sadness, name yr beef but
Pop is eating & is big &
fat — sits, maybe, on
the warpy porch in the
woods, lets son do
all the work — muching
— The little girl black &
ugly like Africa eats
her cone — Old Mule
clops on — Son-Bo
has eye on crossroads
for traffic —, holds reins
loose, they turn, talking,
into Rt 64 — now son

   doesnt even look ahead —
quiet road — Old Mule
is alive just as they, suffers
under same skies, Saturday,
Weekday, Sunday shopping

day, Weekday fieldpull
day, Sunday churchgoing
day — sharing life with
the Jackson family —
they will remember that
old Mule & how it lived
with them & slowly relig-
iously drew them to
their needs, without
thanks, they
will remember the life
& presence of Old Mule
— & their hearts'll cry
— "Old Mule was with
us — We fed him oats —
he was glad & sad
too — then he died —
buried in the mule earth
— forgot — like a
man a mule is <u>& will
be</u> — " Ah North
Carolina (as they turn
into the countrified home
& slowly roll home with
the groceries of the
week scattered on the
platform) — Ah
Saturday — Ah

skies above the gnawing
human scene.

LP Mama slice me one
        of am — slice me
        this kind of am —
        what is this —
            Mama what
            kind is this?
C Swiss!
LP I want Swiss
        Nam nam nam
        (hamburg frying) (radio
        noon) (hot South)

Saturday afternoon in Rocky
Mt. woods — in a tankling
gray coupe the young father
crosses the crossroads with
his 4 dotters piled on the
seat beside him all eyes
— The drowsy store the
great watermelons sit dis-
posed in the sun, on the
concrete, by the fish box,
like so many fruit in
an artist's bowl —
watermelons plain green

& the watermelon with
the snaky rills all
tropical & fat to burst
on the ground — came
from viney bottoms of
all this green fertility —
Behind Fats' little shack,
under waving tendrils
of a pretty tree, the
smalltime Crapshooters
with strawhats & overalls
are shooting for 10¢
stakes — as peaceful &
regardant as deer in
the morning, or New
England boys sitting in
the high grass waiting for
the afternoon to pass.
Paul Blake ambles over
across the road to watch
the game, stands
back, arm on tree,
watching smiling silence.
Cars pull up, men
squat — there goes Jack
to join them, everywhere
you look in the enormity
of this peaceful scene

you see him walking, on
  soft white shoes, bemused
—Last night a few
hotshots & local sailors
on leave grabbed those

reed fishingpoles &
waved them in the drunken
Friday night dark, yelling
"Sturgeon!—catfish!
—Whooee!"—
  They're still unbought
in the old stained
barrell—A trim little
truck is parked, eagerly
at the ice porch, the
farmer's inside having
5 pounds of pork chops
sliced, he likes em for
breakfast—A
hesitant Negro laborer
headed home to his
mother & younger brothers
in the woods is speculating
over a hambone in the
counter—Sweet
life continues in the
breeze, the golden fields—

August senses September
in the deeper light of
its afternoons — senses
Autumn in the brown
burn of the corn, the
stripped tobacco — the
faint singe appearing
on the incomprehensible
horizons — the tanned
  tiredness of gardens, the
cooler, brisker breeze —
  above all the cool
  mysterious nights —

Night — & when the
great rains of the
night boom & thunder
  in the South, when
    the woods are black-
      ened, made wet,
        mudded, shrouded,
        impossibled —

& when the rain
drips from the roof
of the G. Store
in silver tragic milky
beadlets over the bright

bulb-light of the
old platform — inside
we see the snow white
bags of flower, the
whitewashed woodwalls,
the dark & baneful
harness hanging, a
few shining buckets
for the farm —
Sat. rainy night,
the cars come by
raising whizzes of
smoky dew from
the road, their tires
hum, they go off
to a rumble of
   their own —
And the great falls —
The watermelons are
wetted, cooled — The
earth breathes a
new rank cold up
— there's winter
in the bones of this
earth — Thunder of
our ancestors, Blake,
Kingsley, Harris, —
thunder of our ancestors

rumbles in the unseen
  sky—the wood walls
of the store have now
that tragic businesslike
look of hardships in
the old rain, use in
old wars, old necessities
—Now we see that
there were men who
wore raincoats & boots
& struggled here—

& only left their ghosts,
  & these few hardhip
houses, to sit in the
Saturday night rain.
  How different from
the Saturday night of
the cities, the Chinatowns,
the harbors of the
world!—This silent
place haunted by
  corn shapes, the
  beauteous shrouds of
fields, the white leer
flash of lightning, the
stern tones of thunder
(the rattlebones of

bunder, the long buuk
braun roll of munder,
the far off hey - Call
of old poor sunder,)
—Ah South! of
which I read, as a
child, of coonskin caps,
  Civil wars, piney woods,
brothers, dogs, morning
& new hope—Ah
South! Poor America!
The rain has been
falling a long time on
thee & on thy
history—
  George hustles across
the road with a
bagful of his own
beer—a Grandet
of the Americas,
worse than Grandet!
  he wears no miser's
    Puritan cap, or
      gloves, but smoking
      a harmless cigar—

the bulb shines sad
& lonely on the old

wood porch of the
South — I see it —
    In the loam of
the Blake yard sweet
 rain has soaked
   in greens & flowers
   & the grass, & in
   the mud, & sends
 up fragrances of
   the new clean
   eternal Earth —
   Inside the low
   roofed homey rosy
    lit Blake home, see
    the little family
    there, bearing Time
   in a rainy hour
    in the silence of themselves
Leaves thin-shadow on
the wall — on the
mottled redbrick base
foundation — on the
 wet variant tangled
 weeds & up-sway
   grasses of the yard —
   Rain glitters in
     little bark-pools
     of the tree-trunk

—sweet cool night
& washed up, heavy
hanging vegetation
—Lights of passing
cars dance in the
drip-drops of the
awning—Little Paul
muses at the sofa
window, turns &
yells—"Why is
it <u>cause</u>, Daddy, why
is it <u>cause</u>?"

PANORAMIC CATALOG SKETCH
OF BIG EASONBURG
(backyard)

  From right 90° to left
rich brick house where kid
lives who rides pony thru to-
bacco field, farmers say
"Come on, work in the barn"
& his father driving by says
"If you wanta work, that
barn is ready" & he gallops
away saying, "The hell
with work" & niggerfarmers
& pickaninnies in hotfield
chuckle & scratch heads—
Patrician little bitch he is—
his house has big TV antenna,
8 white gables, big
garage, swings, trucks,
Farmall tractor, white iron
  lawnchairs, Bird houses
dog pens, clip't shrubs, lawn,
basketball basket & pole,
—behind house we see
trees & pines of the forest
—a thin scraggle of corn
a 100 feet off—The

dreaming weedy meadow
— then the redroof out-
buildings of Andrews old
  farm — with brick chim
nies, graywood built, ancient,
lost in trees which in clear
late afternoon make glady
black holes for the Sweeny
in the Trees dream of
children — distant rafts
of corn — then the tobacco
curing barn near a
  stick ramp with piled
  twigs or boughs & a redroof
  porch, & a door, <u>smoked</u>,
            at top,
    tho still with old hay

hook for when it once
was a barn (?) — there
too black holes of green
woods — A brand new
flu-cure barn with white tin
roof, new wood, unpainted,
no windows — Then another
old one — over the yellowing
topleaves of the tobacco
field — then the majestic

nest of Great Trees where
homestead sits — darkshaded,
hidden, mystical & ripply-
lit, hints of red roofs,
old gray dark wood,
poles, old chimney, still,
peaceful, mute, with
shadows lengthening along
barnwalls — The trees:
fluffy roundshaped except
for stick tree in middle
forking ugly up, & on
right skeletal of under-
round silhouetting dark
boughs against wall of
forest till round of umbrella
leaftop — Between here
& there I see the rigid
woodpole sticks out of
haystack, conical Stack,
with a cross stick, surrounded
by hedge of weeds, of
brown & gray gold hairy
texture in clear French
Impressionistic Sun —
    After farm solid
wall of forest broken
sharply at road, where

wall resumes on other side
— There is the gray

vision of the old tenant
shack with pale brick
chimbley silhouetted
against a hill-height of
September corn turned
frowsy & hay color —
with mysterious Carolina
continuing distant trees
beyond — & the faintest
wedge of littlecloud right
on horizon above — Across
road forestwall is darker,
deeper, pine trunks stand
luminous in the dark shade
bespotted & specked with
background browngreen
masses — horizontal puff-
green pinebranches, all
over the frizzly corn
top sea — Then Rod's
   logcabin, with pig pen
(old gray clapboards) &
whitewashed barrel & Raleigh
News & Observer mailbox

& telephone pole connecting
up house with 3 strands —
   his withered corn in yard,
   chimney, logs mixed with
white plaster, rococo
   log cabin, horizontal
wood & plaster striped
chimney — Fruit tree in
back waving in faintbrown
of its California — Similar
house of neighbor where stiff
gentleman sits in Panama
hat in Carolina rockchair
   surveying rusticities —

Then, in deepening sha-
dows: - (with him some
women with lap chillun,
Sun-afternoon, breeze, beez
of bugs, hum of cars on
hiway) — Far off in
pure blue an airliner
   lines for Richmond —
— then the yellow diamond
Stop sign, back of it,
with brown wood pole
shadowing across it — A

stand of sweetly stirring
trees & then Buddy Tom's
corn, tall, rippling, talkative,
haunted, gesturing, dogs run
thru it, weeds run riot,
trees protrude beyond —
  Then his whitewashed
  poles, chickencoop, doors,
    hinges, rickety wire —
weeds — wild redflowers —
a tall stately pine
with black balls of
  cone silhouetted against
    keen blue — under
      it an excited weeping
      willow waving like
      a Zephyr song — 2 cars
      parked beneath it, blue
      fishtail Cad — Tom's —
      stiff big red flower —
      folks visitin, talking —
      children — Lillian in
        shorts (big, fat) dumps
        a carton in the rusty
      barrel — The base of
      pine whitewashed — Buddy
      Tom's shed, just & peek
      at interior shelf &

paint can — leaning
rake — Forest wall beyond.

They sit with the gold
on their hair —

* * * * * * * * * * *

SECOND BOOK
AUG.   5,   '52

The diningroom of
Carolyn Blake has
a beautiful hardwood
floor, varnished shiny,
with occasional dark
knots; the rag rug
in the middle is woven
by her mother of the
  historic socks, dresses
    & trousers of the
    Kerouac family in 2
    decades, a weft of
    poor humanity in its
pain & bitterness — The
  walls are pale pink
  plaster, not even pink,

a pink-tinged pastel,
the No Carolina afternoon
aureates through the
white Venetian blinds
& through the red-pink
plastic curtains & falls
upon the plaster, with
soft delicate shades — here,

by the commode in
the corner, profound
underwater pink; then,
in the corner where
the light falls flush,
bright creampink
  that shows a tiny
  waving thread of
  spiderweb overlooked

by the greedy house-
keeper — So the white
paint shining on the
doorframes blends with
the pink & pastel &
makes a restful room.
  The table is of simple
  plytex red surface,
  with matching little
  chairs covered in
  red plastic — But Oh
  the humanity in the
  souls of these chairs,
    this room — no words!
  no plastics to name
    it!

Carolyn has set out
a little metal napkin
holder, with green
paper napkins, in
   the middle of her
   table. Nothing is
provincial — there is
nothing provincial in
America — unless
   it is the radio, static-
ing from late afternoon
   Carolina August
   disturbances — the
   vast cloud-glorious
   Coastal Plain in its
   green peace —

The voices of rustic-
affectated announ-
cers advertising feeds
& seeds — & dull
organ solos in the
radio void — Maybe
   the rusticity of the
province of NC is
   in the pictures on C's
   livingroom wall: 2
   framed pictures of

bird dogs, to please
her husband Paul,
who hunts. A noble
black dog stepping
with the power of a

great horse from a
pond, quail-in-mouth,
with sere Autumns
in the brown swales
& pale green forests
beyond; & 2 noble
nervous white & brown
dogs in a corn-gold
field, under pale
clouds, legs taut, tails
stiff like pickets,
with a frondy sad
glade beyond where
an old Watteau would
  have placed his
misty courtiers book

in hand at Milady's
fat thigh — These
pictures are above the
little dining table —
  Meaningless picturelets

over the bureau in
the other corner (put
 there temporarily
 by finicky Carolyn)
a dull picture of
red flowers & fruit
rioting in the gloom—
 One chair: - a
black high-back
 wood rocker, with
 low seat, styled

in the oldfashioned
country way, hint
of old New England
& Colonial Carolina—
a hint lost to the
static of the radio
& the hum & swish
of the summer fan
set on the floor to
circulate air in a
wide arc from one
 extreme twist of
 its face to the
other—a fan
brought home by her
 husband from his

office at the Telephone
Company.
    CB herself, cig in
mouth, is opening the
windows behind the
  blinds — she'd closed
   them at 9 o'clock
  AM to keep the
  morning freshness in
— & now, near 4,
  the air cooling,
  she opens them again
 — a fan can
only stir dusts of
 the floor — Instantly
scents of fields

& trees comes into the
pink room with the
hardwood floor — A
gay wicker basket
is on the floor be-
neath the windows,
 full of newspapers
  & magazines & a
Sears Roebuck cata-
logue — CB is
wearing shorts, sandals

& a nondescript vest-
shirt — just did her
housework — washed
the lunch dinners
<u>&</u> is about to take a

bath — The breeze
of afternoon pillows
in the redpink plas-
tic curtains. Carolyn
Blake stands, cig in
mouth, glancing briefly
at the yard outside
— beyond it stretches
a meadow, a corn
  field, a tobacco
  field, & faintly
  beyond the wreckage
  of a gray flu-
    curing barn the
  wall of the forest
  of the South.

CB is a thin, trim
little woman of 33 —
looking younger, with
cut bangs, short hair,
bemused, modern —

On her commode, two
shelves above a drawer
& opening hinged door,
pale wood, is a
wooden salad bowl,
upright; two China
plates, upright; an
earthen jug of
Vin Rosé, empty,
  brought from NY
  by her mother;

a green glass dish —
for candy — a glass
ashtray — & two
brass candle holders
— these things lumi-
nescent in the glow
from the windows,
in still, fan-buzzing,
lazy Carolina afternoon
time. On the
radio a loud pro-
longed static from
nearby disturbances
rasps a half
minute —
    On the wall

above the husband's
diningtable chair
hangs a knickknack
shelf, with 3 levels,
  tiny Chinese vase
  bowl with cover —
copper horse eques-
trian & still in its
petite mysterious
  shelf — & Chinese
porcelain rice-girl
with hugehat &
double baskets.
  These are some of
  the incidental
  appurtenances in
  the life of a little

Carolina housewife
in 1952.

She turns & goes into
the parlor — a
more elegant room,
with green leather
chairs, gray rug, book
shelves, — goes to the
screen door — lets

in Little Paul &
Little Jackie Lee —
Her son Little Paul comes
  yells "Mommy I
wants some ice water!
Me & Jackie Lee wants
    some ice water!
  Mommy!" She shoos
  them in with an ab-
  sentminded air —
  Little Paul, blond, thin,
  is her son; Jackie Lee,
  dark, plumper, belongs
  to a neighbor — They
  rush in, barefooted,
  each 4, in little
  shorts, screaming,
  wiggling —
      In the kitchen, at
her refrigerator she
pours out ice

cube trays — Little
Paul holds the green
plastic waterbottle —
  "That water's warm,"
says Carolyn Blake,
"let me make you

some ice — "
     "I wants some
cracked ice Mommy!
 Is that what you
 wants Jackie Lee?"
     "Ah-huh," — assent,
"Ah-huh Pah-owl."
     The little mother
gravely works on the
ice; above the sink,
 with a crank, is an
  ice cracker; she

jams in the ice cubes,
standing tip toe
reaches up & cranks
it down into a red
plastic container;
wiggling the little boys
wait & watch — The
kitchen is modern &
clean — She slowly
goes about taking down
small glasses from
a cupbord, jams the
 crushed ice in them.
     They clasp the
     glasses & rush off —

to Little Paul's
bedroom.

"This is our home, that
trailer's our home,"
says Little Paul as
  they wrangle over
    a toy trailer-truck
  on the white chenille
    bedspread.
      They have toy horses,
    "Now you kill yrs."
    "Kill <u>yours</u>" — Jackie
    "He's killed."
    "Arent you glad?"
    "They aint nothing
but big bad wolves . . .

Hey — mine's got a
broken leg."
      "Give it to me."
      "They're not <u>your</u>
horses!"
      An incredible
city of toys in the
corner, on a card
table, a big doll
house, garages, cranes,

clutters of card,
accordions, silos,
dogs, tables, cash
registers, merry
  go rounds with

insignia goldhorses,
marbles, airplanes,
an airport —
     Little Paul —
"Here — here's $12
for those horses,"
  striking cashregister,
   Jackie: "12 dollars?"
  The bedroom has
pastel green walls;
the crib in the corner's
now only for toys —
Polo Pony for water,
  a balloon; rubber
    naked doll; black
lamb — At foot
of bed a hamper
full of further toys —
On a little table
with flowery tablecloth
a small standing
library of Childrens

books—A huge
double bed, four posts,
  the little Prince
gets up on it &
walks around—
  He opens the
hamper, "Jackie!
  know what? I
  found a rake!"

Holding toy rake.
"You can work on
the track."
  On the open hamper
cover they hammer
  their horses. "This
is gonna be a
horse race." Paul
finds a track from
his Lionel Train box.
  "Are they glad?"
  "Yes."
  "Here comes another
straight track!"
—to distinguish from
curve tracks—

"Dont let em go
Jackie!" he calls
from the track
box.

"I wont."
"Ding ding ding!"
shouts Paul pounding
with a railroad stop
sign on the hamper.
"Ding ding racehorse!
Ding ding track!"
Jackie: "One of em's our
main horse!"
"Huh?"
"This one's our
main horse."
"Pah-owl the
horses are goin out
in the tunnel! — "
"The train's not
comin down that
way. I better
make a turn race.
No — " adjusting
curvetrack to straight
track — "no, gotta
git anodder race
track — You

better help me
    Jackie."

"Why?"
"Cause—Cause
this is a hard track.
Sure. Sure is.
Now let me put a
track right here.
Hard. This hard."
    "Now it's goin
right around that
    tunnel. Paul we're
gonna have a whole
    lot. We have
    crow-co-dals—"
    "If you mess up
that train track
one more—I'll

shoot ya!"
Jackie: "Talkin to me?"
Paul: "Shoo—flooshy you."
    Outside, in gold
day, the weeping
willows of Buddy Tom
Harris hang heavy
& languid & beauteous

in the hour of life;
the little boys are
not aware of
God, of Universal
Love, & the vast
earth bulging in
the sun — they
are a part of
the swarming mystery
  and of the salvation
— their eyes reflect
humanity & intelli-
gence —
    In the kitchen the
little mother, letting
them play, bustles
& bangs around for
supper. Something
  in the air presages
  the arrival of the
    father old man —
Soft breeze puffs
  the drapes in Paul's
room as he & Jackie
wriggle on the floor
    "Hey Jackie — you
  got it on the wrong way
        aint ya? Now

put this in the back
—now fix it.
(Singing) I think
I'll get on this train,
I think I'll get
on that train,
I think I'll get
on the ca-buss.
Broom! briam!"
   lofting his wood
   plane—screaming—
"Eee- yall—
gweyr!" On
   his belly, smiling,—
   suddenly thinking
     silently . . .

In the kitchen
changed to yellow
tailored shorts,
   tailored gray vest
   shirt, & white san-
dals the little housewife
prepares supper. She
stands at the white
tile sink washing the
small squash under
the faucet—prelim-

inary maneuvers for
a steak supper she
decided upon at the
last minute —
   "Hello Geneva —
he went to Henderson this
noon — I _think_ he'll
be back — bye — "
— She slices them into
a glass bowl, standing
idly on one foot
with the other out-
   thrust at rest —
   the little boys now
   playing outside —
   The screendoor
   slams out front —
   "Hey!" cries
   CaB not moving from
      her work
      "Hey Moe" greets
   her husband —

He comes into the
kitchen, Panama
   hat, white shirt, tie
— casual — tall,
   husky, blond, hand-

some — smooth moving,
slow moving, relaxed
Southerner — He
has mail & that after-
noon at his mother's
house in Henderson
50 miles away, while
on a business trip for the
tel. co., he went
thru his grandmother's
trunk & found old
letters & a pair of
old diamond studded

cuff links, he stands
in the middle of the
kitchen reading the
old letter — written
by a lost girl to
his uncle Ed also
now lost — the sadness
of long lost enthusiasms
on ruled paper, in
pencil —
But now a storm
is coming — "It's
gonna storm," says
Jack — From the

west the ranked
forward-leaning
clouds come parading
—stationary puff
clouds of the calm
are snuffed &
taken up—From
the East big black
thunderhead with
his misty gloom
forms hugeing—
   Directly above

   the embattled roof
of the Blake's the
   sea of dark has
   formed—the first
   light snaps—the
   first thunder crackles,
   rolls, & suddenly
   drops to the bottom
   with a shake-earth
   boom—More &
      more the rushing
   clouds are gray, a
      forlorn airplane in
      the southeast hurries

home — Far in
the northeast

the remnant after-
noon's still soft
& fleecy gold, still
rich, calm, clouds
still make noses &
have huge maws
of incomprehensible
comedy in their
sides — Thunder
travels in the West
heavens — "parent
power dark'ning in
the West" — A
straycloud hangs
upsidedown & helpless
in the thunderhead
glooms, still retaining
white —

Mrs. Langley nextdoor
swiftly removes her
sheets & wash from
the wire line — looks
around timidly —
absent in her work,

frowning in the glare,
peaceful in the
   stillness before storm
   (as one birdy tweets
   in the forest across
   to the North) — Grass,
   flowers, weeds wave
   with dull expectancy
—The first spray
   drops wetten the
      little Langley girl
      in her garden

play—"Hey" she
says—Children
call from all sides
   as the rain begins
      to patter—Still
      a bird sings.
      Still in the NE
      the clouds are
   creampuff soft &
      afternoon dreamy.
      Some blues show
      in the horizon grays
—Now the rain
   pelts & hums—
      gathers to a wind—

a hush — a mighty
wash — the

trees are showing
signs of activity —,
the corn rattles,
  the wall of the
  forest is dimmed
  by smokeshroud
  rains — a solitary
  bee rises, the
    road glistens. It
is hot & muggy. Cars
  that come from
up the road roll on
    their own sad images
    gray & dumb —
The cooling thirsting
    earth sighs up a
  cucumber freshness
mixed with steams
    of tar & warp danks
    of wood — Toads
    scream in the meadow
    ditch, the Harris rooster
    crows. A new
      atmosphere like the
      atmosphere of screened

porches in Maine in
   March, on cold
      gray days; &
not like sunny Carolina
      in July, is seen
      thru the windows
      above the kitchen
      sink: dark wet
      leaves are shaking
   like iron. A tiny

ant pauses to rub
its threads on a
   spine of leaf—
the fly solemnly
jumps from the
bedspread to the
screen hook—as
breezes rush into
   the house from that
   perturbed West.
      "Close that door!"
   cries the mother—
      doors slam—
      "Paul I said you
         stay here!"

          Rain nails kiss
          the dance of the shiny
                        road.

The parched tobacco is
   dark as grass.
   Behind the storm the
   blue reappears — it was
      just a passing shower —
   CB doesnt even bother
   to close her windows.
      Inside an hour the
grass is almost dry
again, vast areas of
open blue firmament
show the cottonball
   horizons low & bright
   over the darknesses
   of the pine wall woods,
up the road in clean
white shirt & pale over-
   alls that looked
   almost washed by the
   rain, comes the pure
   farmer, a Negro,
limping, as orgones dance
   in the electric washed
   new air.

All is well in
Rocky Mount, North
  Carolina, as 5 o'clock
  in the afternoon shudders
on a raindrop leaf,
& the men'll be coming
home.

AVILA BEACH, CALIF.
(WRITTEN YEAR LATER)
———————————————

Seethe rush
longroar of sea
  seething in floor
  of sand — distant
  boom of world
  shaking breakers
— sigh & intake
of sea — income,
outgo — rumors
of sea —
  hushing in air —
    hot rocks
  in the sand —
  the earth shakes
    & dances to the
  boom — I think

I hear propellers
of the big union
oil Tanker
warping in at
pier — A great
lost rock sits
upended on
the skeely sand
— — Who the
fuck cares

* * * * * * * * * * * * * *

1954 RICHMOND HILL SKETCH ON VAN WYCK BOULEVARD

Before my eyes I see
"Faultless Fuel Oil" written
in white letters on a green
board, with "11-30" in
small numbers on each
side to indicate the street
address of the company.
The building is small,
modern, redbrick, square,
with curious outjutting
new type triangular

screens that I cant really
examine from this side
of the boulevard but look
like protection from
oldfashioned robbers &
stones — The garage door
  entrance for the oil
    trucks: green. The

building sits upon the
earth under a gray
radiant sky — I see
vague boxes in the right
front window — Cars
are going by with a
sound like the sea in
the superhiway below it
— It is very bleak
& I only give you the
  picture of this bleakness.
  By bleakness I mean:
  unnatural, stiff, lost
  in a void it cant
  understand, — in a
  void to which it has no
  relation because of the
  transiency of its function,

to earn money by deliv-
ering oil. But it has

a neat Tao of its
own. In any case this
<u>scene</u> is of no interest
to me. & is only an
example. A <u>scene</u>
should be selected by
the writer, for haunted-
ness-of-mind interest.
  If you're not haunted
  by something, as by a
    dream, a vision, or
  a memory, which are
    involuntary, you're not
interested or even involved.

SKETCH WRITTEN IN OUELLETTE'S
LUNCH IN LOWELL MASS. 1954

"Ya rien plus pire qu'un
enfant malade—
  a lava les <u>runs</u> — j'aita assez découragez
  j brauilla avec—"
"Un ti peu d <u>gravy</u>*
d tu?" — "Staussi bien . . . Mourire

chez nous que mourire
  la" — "L'matin
yava les yieux griautteux"
— "J fa jama deux
  journée d'suite" —
    "J mallez prende
une marche — " "Comme
qui fa beau apramidi ha?"

"A tu lavez les vites?"
— "J ai lavez toute les
vites du passage" —
    "Qui mange dla
marde"
    "A lava les yeux
pochées — tsé quand
  qu'on s leuve des foit?"

CAT SKETCH ON THE CONCORD RIVER
(1954)

The Perfect Blue Sky
is the Reality, all 6
Essential Senses abide
  there in perfect
  indivisible Unity
    Forever — but

here down on the
stain of earth the
ethereal flower in
our minds, dead
cats in the Concord,
it's a temporary
middle state be-
  tween Perfection of
the Unborn & Per-
  fection of the
    Dead—the Restored
  to Enlightened
Emptiness—Compromise
me no more, "Life"
—the cat had no
self, was but the
  victim of accumu-
lated Karma, made
by Karma, removed
  by Karma (death)
—What we
  call life is just
  this lugubrious
  false stain in the
  crystal emptiness
—The cat in waters
"hears" Diamond

Samadhi, "sees"
Transcendental Sight—

"smells" Trans. odor,
"tastes" Trans. taste,
"feels" Trans. feeling,
"thinks" Trans. thot
    the one Thot
  —So I am not
  sad for him—
                Concord River RR
                Bridge
                Sunday Oct 24 '54
                Lowell
                5 PM
    A ridiculous N E
  tumbleweed danced
across the RR Bridge

  Thoreau's Concord
is blue aquamarine
in October red
  sereness—little
Indian hill towards
Walden, is orange
    brown with Autumn—
    The faultless sky
  attests to T's solemn

      wisdom being correct
— but perfect Wisdom
   is Buddha's
Today I start teaching
by setting the example
not words only

ROCKY MOUNT 1952 (again) WHILE
HITCH HIKING BACK FROM NORFOLK VA.

   "You done lost the
man's hole . . . Smart
   Alex."

N.C. — Near Woodland N.C.
Hams hanging by wild
   bulb-bugs in hot
   N.C. nite — sad dust
   of driveway, scattered
   softdrink hot-day
   bottles, old crates
   sunk in earth for
   steps, pumps (Premium
   & Pure Pep) —

hillbilly music in car
— trucks growling
thru — old tire,

rake — old concrete
block — old bench —
& tufts of green
grass seen au bord du
  chemin quand les
  machines passes —
    L —

* * * * * * * * * * *

ROCKY MOUNT CAR SHOP (RAILROAD)

  Yard in afternoon of
  August — bright red
drum shining in bright green
& yellow grass-weeds, buds, —
  old used rusty brakeshoes
    & parts piled —

Sooty old woodwarp
ramp — in weeds —
fat RR clerk with
baseball hat walking
across, cigar, scratching
head, removing hat —
will go home to dogs,
  radio, wife, blond boy
on a tricycle in white
bungalow — Old A.C.L.

Railway Exp Ag. 441
        weather-brown
        Cracked cars—2, 3
of them—nameless
parts arranged in
weeds by tired Negro
workers—Puff sweet
Carolina clouds in sultry
blue over head—my
eyes smarting from fresh
paint in office, from
  no sleep—drowsy
office like school days,
with sleepy rustles of
    desk papers & lunch-in-
    the-belly—hate it—
SP is in cool, dry
Western, romantic Frisco
of bays—with—
  hills of purple eve &
  mystery—& Neal
  ——here is fuzzy,
  unclear, hot, South,
  hot turpentined poles
  at tracks that lead

to Morehead City, Sea &
  Africa—& <u>impossible</u>

<u>lead</u> tho—just dull
fat cops & people in
heat—Easonburg is
better.

DIDNT HAVE PENCIL with
  me to sketch the
    bluebells that climb
  up from beautiful
  fields of weeds to
  curl around the old
    dead cornstalk that
    is rattly crackly
    deadbone & wreaths
    it purple, softens it,
     gives it a juicier
        (THE WOODS ARE SHINING)
  sound in the wind,
  droops it, embraces
  it, gives it the
    Autumn kiss for
    harvest stack farewell
—old Melancholy Frowse
is wound round in
    Carolina in the
    Morning—
      The piercing blue of
  the first Autumn

day, the woods
are shining, the
Nor'east wind making
ripples in the
flooded tarns — all
is lovely this Sunday morn.
The Weeping Willow
no longer hangs but
waves ten thousand
goodbyes in the
direction of the wind
— The clean
little tele. pole without
crossbars stands lost
in Carolina vegetations,
some of the corn half
its height, & that
lush forest of
Carolina backs it
solemnly & with
a promise — that
was here for boys killed
in Palau in 1944, boys —

that had sisters who
yet mourn this Sun.
morning — hope
that was there for

the strange Cherokee
—& now for me
that wanders round
my earth — amen.

Sitting in the middle
of the woods with
Little Paul, Princey
& Bob—Little foxy
Prince sits panting
—big mosquitos—
Big Bob panting
hard, tongue out,
licks his mouth,
blinks eye, big
tongue flapping over
sharp teeth—
drooling—Pine
needle floor is
brown, dry cracky
odorless—
blue sky
is sieve above
tangled dry
vining green heart
leafing trunking
cobwebbing—
now & then sway

massedly in upper
winds — Sun
makes joy gold
spots all over
—

The sand road
is blinding old —
many gnats —
cars raise storms
of dust — wind
sways grass

in ditch ridges —
straight thinpines
stand in vaulty
raw blue, clean —
Negroboys bike
by smiling —
Princey's little
wet nose —
no more — no more —
Oh Princey, Bob,
Little Paul, woods
of Easonburg, no more
— (freedom of
the blue cities calls
me.)

SHORT TIC SKETCHES (TICS ARE FLASHES OF MEMORY OR DAYDREAM)

(1) Hartford — when I was
a boy poet & wrote
for myself — no
frantic fear of "not
being published," but
the joy, the shining
morning, "This love
of mine" — leaves,
houses, Autumn — and
  Immortality
(2) Hospital, 1951, letting
  the images overwhelm
  me, not rushing out
    to lasso them &
      getting all pooped
      out — NOW Coach
(3) Oh when I was young &
had a pretty little Edie
in bright lavender
sweater to hug to
me — big breasts, thighs
warm, bending-to-me waist,
— now I'm cold as
  the moon . . . no more women
    for puffy-eyed Jack —

who once posed in a
button-down boy sweater
for a picture — When —
O when, reading the N.Y.
Times, he thought he
was learning everything —
& has learned but decay
   only — & sadness of partings —

(4) Mr Whatsisname
in beat ragged coat
 in r.r. office, has same
haggard anxious soul-
 neglected sorrow as
 he searches among
 ledgers, mouth open,
 as my father in his
 shop of old yore —
     with glasses on
 nose, blue eyes, —
   O doom, death,
 come get me! I cannot
live but to remember
 — old puff lined
Jack, go put a
 poor blanket of
    dirt over your
     noble nose.

Last night, under the
stars, I saw I belonged
among the big poets
    (did I read that somewhere?)

        ————————
         —————

(5) Raw, almost childlike
slowmotion dinosaur
  ideas of 1947
  bop on So. Main
  L.A. — "You Came
  To Me From out of
  Nowhere" — The
  ideas of serious basic
  thinkers, young, energetic,
  powerful — joy comes
  from the really new —
    Bird was like that, but
    more & most complex

Be like Bird, find y.self
  little story tunes to
string yr. complexities
  along a wellknown line
or you will sound like
  a crazy Tristano of

the Seymour-record
(Bartok — Bar Talk)
(Bela BarTalk)
— Bird has visions between
bridges — So do you
 in visions between chapter
lines — —!!!
   Shakespeare, Giroux's
Shakespeare Opera
Books — <u>simple</u> — not
<u>that</u> simple but use
story-forms — or phooey,
 do what you please —

Never will be bored in the
bottom — at the hut, the
 secret room, the weed,
 the mind — the daVinci
   series —
—
   I was in my mother's
house, in winter — I was
writing "The Sea is My
 Brother" — what have
I learned since then?
 I have written <u>Doctor</u>
<u>Sax</u> since last prattling
like this —

NEAR SANDY CROSS N.C.

Quiet shady
sand road at
late afternoon, a
crick pool-like
 & ripple reflecting
& brown with
froth spit motion-
 less, & exotic
 underwater leaves,
& tangled jungly
banks under dry
old board bridge
—vined sides of it
—a wild claw
tree protruding from
 silent greeneries—
 with 12 agonies

of fingers, & one
twisted guilty body,
 the weatherbeaten bark
as clean as a
woman's good thigh,
 with a climb of
 vines on it—The
 brown & tragic
 cornfield shining in

the late sun up the
road — The clearing,
the negros, the
    flu barn, the white
    horse nibbling —
        Coca Cola sign at
    the lonely golden
    little bend — a cricket

I got up this road
into my Maturity

    — — — — — — —

And what will that
    corn do for you?
— will it soothe you
& put you to bed
        at night? Will
        it call yr name
    when winter blows?
        Or will it just
    mock the bones
        of yr. skeleton,
        when August
            browning breaks
    its Silence camp,
        & blows —
        Immortality just

passed over me
— in these woods
— as it cooled —
 & darked — at
 6 PM —
The Angel visited me &
    told me to go on

—

THESE Mornings in A.C.L.
office will be remembered
as happy — the visionary
  tics, the dreams, the delicate
  sensations — must be
  that way on the road
  of rock & rail.

Repeat — let it come
to you, dont run after it
— It would be and _is_ like
running after sea waves —
to embrace them up where
you stand when you catch
them — aïe —
<u>TICS</u>
    The long dismal winter
street where I'd go to see
Grace Buchanan — & Mary —

(The prophet is without
         honor in his own family.)
    A "tic" is a sudden thought
that inflames & immediately
    disappears—
       The Indians see a Little
Cloud a Shining Traveller
         in the Blue Sky

TIC
       The yard with the
       brothers & dogs in the
       rickety back of Ozone
       Park back of Aqueduct track
       —Why' is it have to be Kentucky?

                  * * *

The Time-type executive
—"Ahuh,—yeah—
That would be about
500 kegs a month—
Well alright if
that takes care of
yr situation thats
what they want I
expect—Yeah—
  hm—We'll try to do
  that this afternoon

—anything you want
just holler—ah huh—
—bye—same to
you"—click—

TICS
O fogs of South City,
the rumble of the drag,
outside, chicory coffee,
the doom-wind-sheds
of Armour & Swift—
  waybills in the Night—
the clean mystery
of California—these
sensations—Why makes
it me shudder to remember,
if it aint <u>hanted</u>—

    The exams in University
    Gym—Bill Birt, morning—
    <u>those</u> smells, sensations,

rise to me from just
standing at requisition
shelf where fresh paint
& cool breeze blow—usually
rouses Frisco RR work—
Why?—if not hanted,

charged materially with
substances that are
    locked in (and as
        Proust says waiting to be
        unlocked.) Ah I'm
        happy — Yet it's only
            11:30 & Time Crawls —
            & I'm so sick of the
burden time, everything's
        already happened, why
            not <u>happen</u> all at
            once, the charge in
            one shot —
Old clerk to other old
clerk — 25 yrs. same
place — "What are you
    today, Columbus?" —
as he searches lost ledger
— Sad? It's abominable

— The names of old
lost Bigleaguers Cudworth
used to paste in his books —
    1934, 1933 — Dusty Cooke,
    lost names — lost suns —
        as more sad than rain —
        — those 2 men drinking
at the old bar on Third

     & alley — old Meeks
       Bar 1882 — why do I think
     of them? — Pa & Charley
     Morrissette spectralizing
        Frisco-Lowell —

ROCKY MOUNT oldstreet
with 90 year old Buffalo
Bill housepainter spitting
brown 'bacca juice on
roof, — & younger painter
who heartbreakingly white-
washes that part near the
    porch reminds me of poor
    lost Lowell — And old
    lady sewing little boy
    bluepants on historic
    porch breaks my heart —
    & old black bucket &
    fire in negroyard & little
    gal in scrabble reminds
    me Mexico & the Fella-
    heen peoples I love —
        for old retired couple on
        that porch aint just
        sittin in the sun, sit
        in judgment & Western

         hatred — not all
                of em —

                   I am alone
in Eternity with my Work
      For
         as I sat on the
burnt out stump on
the Concord River bank
staring into the flawless
  blue & thinking of
  earth as a stain,
suddenly I realized
the utter absurdity of
my squatting assy
    humanity too, the
    infinitely empty
crock of form, like
  suddenly hearing myself
sneeze in the quiet
Street night & it
sounds like somebody
  else — Therefore, is
my pelvic ambition
for girl's bone-cover
the True Me? — or
is it not, like the

sneeze & the ass,
<u>absurd</u>, like the
   smell of the shit
   of a saint

THE GREAT FALL is
rumbling in America —
   in back of the Tele-
phone office in R.M. you
  can see it in the profounder
  blue of the late aft sky
    as seen from among
    the downtown Southern
    redbricks — in the
    brown tips of leaves
    on trees over the garage
    wall — The wholesale
    hardware wall — in the
      particular cold deep red
      that has suddenly
        come into the tobacco
        warehouse roof with
        its spotted loft-
        windows — inside,
          faintly in the

brown like Autumn to-
bacco brown, the piles

of bacco baskets —
Here watching Paul's car I
sit — poised for the
continent again, Aug. 27 '52
And in San Jose the
Great Fall is tangled
brown among the
greens of sun valley
trees, deep shadows
of morning make the
woodfence black
    against the golden
    flares of sere grass —
    California is always
    morning, sun, & shade
— & clean —

lovely motionless green
leaves — vague
plaster rocks lost in
  fields — the dazzling
  white sides of houses
  seen thru the tangly
  glade branches —
  the dry solemn ground
  of California fit for
  Indians to sleep on
— the cardboard

beds of hoboes along
the S.P. track up at
  Milpitas — & the
  clean blue deep
  night at Permanente,
  the dogs barking under
    clear stars, the

locomotive flares
  his big hot orange
  fire on sleeping
  houses in the glade
— sweet California —
memories of Marin
  & the California night
are true & real —
& were right

      And then I went
South to Mexico

      And then I went North
to New York

      To New York, to the
      Apple, New York

(Remember, this isnt chronological)

Mexico December '52

    Plant without growth
in Vegetable bleakness

The thirst, the mournfulness

The terrible benzedrine
depression after big
night of drinking on
  Organo St. with
  La Negra & the
  courtdancer queer
  children after whore
  sluffed me & I lost
  brakeman's lantern,
  French dictionary,

earmuff hat, money,
pages of writing,
  left piss in my
new pots & walked
  off—long rides
  in perfect Mexico
  on bus, sad—but
  at Tamazunchale
  begin to feel good &
see Kingdoms & homes

& heavy syrup air
    of jungle —
& at Brownsville
Missouri Pacific bus — &
    then VICTORIA

"SIRONIA" —
my walk — miss't
 bus — saw Xmas
in rose brown
  r.r. track
  windows —
Sweet stars —
    presaging months
    in Winter 1953
    Richmond Hill at
Ma's house writing
   gemlike
        LOVE
            IS
              SIXTEEN

After which flew
back to Coast to
work mountains
  at San Luis Obispo
puttin up & down

pops — ending I
sail out the Golden
Gate on a Japan
bound freighter that
first goes to New
Orleans where I
drink & take off
("Worlds Champion
shipjumper," says
Burroughs) & return
NY in summer, to
heat & Subterraneans

& Alene Love
& eventual
RAILROAD EARTH
book of Fall
Come - Christmas
O rushing
life,
restless gyre,
seas, cots,
beds, dreams,
sleeps, larks,
starlights, mists,
moons, knowns —

SKETCHES WRITTEN IN ST. LOUIS-TO-NEW YORK AIRPLANE

Winter in No. America,
the sun is falling
feebly from the
South.

Getting rooked of all
my money trying to
get home for Xmas
in time — for a
childhood chimera
blowing all my pay —
flying TWA — Lemme
see, can I find
Jay Landesman's
saloon?
it's going to be
a Merry Xmas
one way or the
other
—————

Winter in No. America,
the passengers on the
right in the TWA plane
have a sea of incandes-
cent milk blinding

in their eyes, from
where the feeble
South American sun
comes raying, plus
  the dazzling sun
  ball herself, but
  on the left, on eastbound
58 out of St. Louis,
  on the fireman's
  side, they see the pale
  blue North out the
  window, also blinding,
    but more seeable—

It's like facing the
  snow on the North side
  of the train eastbound
  in the morning, in a
  strange New England
  of snow created by the
  ice-cap of overcast
  covering the Eastern
  lake & seaboard—
  like Greenland, from
  the top of one of
  its highest coastal
  mountains seeing
  below the enormity

of the continental
inland polar snow
field a thousand,
two thousand miles long

a field of clouds,
no buttercups there;
a glacier of
fiery mad vapor
extending in the
air sea. Down
on the world Premier
Mossadegh cried.
Notre Dame, Terre
Haute, Africas
below. Unbelievable
endless solid floor
of clouds.

        *   *   *   *   *   *   *   *

SOUNDS IN THE WOODS

Karagoo Karagin
criastoshe, gobu,
bois-cracke, trou-or,
boisvert, greenwoods
beezy skilliagoo
arrange-câssez,

cracké-vieu,
green-in buzz
  bee grash—
    Feenyonie
    feenyom—
      Demashtado
    ——Greeazzh—
    Grayrj—

Or—where a festive
fly makes a blade
of grass snap—
Or—Hurried ant
  flies over a leaf—
Or—Deserted village
  clearing of my sit
  Or—I am dead
    Or—I am dead
    because everything
    has already happened
I must go ahead
beyond this dead
to—
      the ground

  to—
      the vast
  to—

                  the moss of the
                  Babylon woodstump
        to —
                  mysterious destruction
        from —
                        blisters
                        bellies
                          stockings
                             fingers with hair
                          tans
                             sores
                                muddy shoes
        Seulement pas, S.P. —
        Aoo reu-reu-reu-
            a bee —

The Woods Are Ave of Me

    Ant town antics
        Joan is dead
        The flup fell down
    I have an ant
        criolling thru
            the rot
              stump
        "Yey" voice
    of <u>human</u> child
    "oh! — " Zzzz

Finally: -
　　Degradled fling lump
　　stick stump motion
　　bump in the brother
　　mump of—
　　　skreeee—lump—
　　　Terre vert—
　　　sflux—seeee—
　　　Spuliookatuk—
　　　Speetee-vizit,
　　　　vizit (bird)—
　　　Vush! the whole
　　　　forust! Zhaam
　　　Sabaam Vom—
　　　V-a-a-m—
　　　R-a-o-o-l—
　　　　m-n-o-o-l-
　　　　z-oo—ZZAY—

Tickaluck—(Funny)
fiddledegree—R-R-
R-R-Rising vrez
　　Zung blump
　　dee-dooo-domm—
　　Deelia-<u>hum</u>—
　　　Bara<u>l</u>idoo—
　　　Spitipit—spitipit—
　　　Ahdeeriabum, ah

grey—
    Vee!
    Eee-lee-lee-
mosquilee—
      Rong big bong
     bee bong—
Atchap-pee
Atchap-pee
Skior! Viz!
Sit!
   Deria-po-<u>pa</u>!
Hit-ta-
   tzi-po-teel,
Te de li a bo—
   Vit! chickalup!

Oooeeeuoom
    Vazzh—
     V-a-z-z
Flip flip flip flup
   Bung ground terre

Doo-ri-oo-ri-oo-ra

Zee—
   Krrrrrr—r-o-t
  Crick
   Fueet!?

Fueet!?

_ _ _ _ _

Written in Easonburg
woods, at one point naked,
Sunday,   Aug 10   1952
— The Sounds of the Woods

PARANOIA AND OIL

When Buz Sawyer
goes to South America
representing Americans
who only think in
terms of paranoia & oil.
— bkfast. in the
  best hotel is only a
  time to read the paper,
  across the park it's
  empty & just a
  paranoiac Indian
    photographer — he
    talks over the
    phone with Mr Boss,
    avoids women —
        Woogh!

WATSONVILLE, CALIF.

Mechanized Saturday
          night — the foggy
Watsonville Main Drag on
the Mexican side has
people on the sidewalks
milling but Mexican field
& section hands dismally
knowing they cant find
love till they return to
Mexico, just wander, &
mostly look into workclothes
stores (!) like I do and
  a group of anxious Indians
  finished with the beet
  & lettuce season have
  bought an enormous suit-
  case at the Army Navy
  store & are going home
    to stern fathers

& good mothers who
have taught them
gentleness & the Virgin
Mother so they dont
clack around wise guys
like the Mexican American

Pachucos — but only
have great sad eyes
searching into the lost
blue eyes of America,
& in the "American"
part of the Main Drag
there are no people,
empty sidewalks, empty
pink neons for bars
  (like Sunnyvale) just
  cars in the street — a
  mechanized Saturday,

with occupants who
look anxiously out for
companionship of Sat
  nite mill crowds but
  the steel of the
  machines is walling them
  off — argh!
    Meanwhile I dig
the woman in her
  sad furnished room above
  Mex Mainstreet, her
  little boy in window
  looking out on the white-
  ness & mystery of
  Nov. 8, 1952 — & the

old wood building's been
covered at front with
plaster — She's in the
window in her pink
dress, radiant, transparent,
lost — I would be
great if I could just
sit in a panel truck
sketching Main Streets
of world — will do.
God will save me
for what I do now,
help my Mom —
he will —

In his idealistic youth on
railroad in Maine Old Bull
says "Why should I have a
radio when I can hear
the music of a crackling fire
& the steam engines in
the yard?" — railroad Thoreau
— he sits alone in his
caboose, in the dark, with
the fire, drinking — Old
Bull Baloon the Man
of America — Guillaume
Bernier of Gaspé —

& says "All that
matters is the healthy
color of that fire" —
but too much bottle,
not enough sottle, brings
him to his last late
years—

TITLE: - THE MORTAL UGLINESS
The Mortal Story
(Haunted Ugly Angles of Mortality)

Did I ever get my
kicks as a kid with
date pie & whipt cream
combining with "Shrine
North South All star
football game Christmas
night in the Orange Bowl"
— dug sports then
as something rich
& at its peak on
holidays when
it went with turkey
dinners & peach shortcake
— Also, remember

the joyous snowy morn-
ings when you played
Football Game Board
with Pop & Bobby
   Rondeau? — the oranges
& walnuts in a bowl,
   the heat of the house,
   the Xmas tinsel on
   the tree, the boys
of the Club throwing
snowballs below
corner Gershom —
   Moody? —
         On the Road _that_
if you will, Sex
   Generation _that_
   if you will —

Made Sick by The Night

My Father Was a Printer

      The trouble with
      fashions is you want
      to fuck the women
      in their fashions
      but when the time
      comes they always

take them off so
they wont get
wrinkled.

Face it, the really
great fucks in a
young man's life was
  when there was no
  time to take yr.
  clothes off, you
  were too hot & she
  was too hot — none
of yr. Bohemian leisure,
this was middleclass
explosions against
  snowbanks, against
  walls of shithouses
  in attics, on sudden
  couches in the lobby —
    Talk about yr. hot peace

****

Marion, <u>Ark</u>.
Earl
Bald Knob
Conway
Russellville
Ozark
Fort Smith
Sallisaw, <u>Okla</u>.
Warner
Muskogee

Austin
Carson City
Meyers, <u>Calif</u>.
Placerville
Sacramento
Lodi
Stockton
Tracy
Livermore
Mission San Jose
SAN JOSE
   1047 E. Santa Clara St.

The Sea is My Brother —
a figment of the gray
sea & the gray America,
of my childhood dreams —

Walked from Easonburg
on old walking-road but
3 miles — in gray thrilling —
with bag — saw Negro
pulled by a mule on a
  bike! — to junction 64,
  immediate ride young hot-
rod speedsters to Spring
Hope, pickt up Wake
  Forest boy too — he
  got off, went downroad
— Hotrod told, as he
went 90, of man
tried pass truck hit

school child & turned
over — Old thin bum
  at S Hope, hitching east,
  from Atlanta, "Almost
  got stuck in old car 10
  miles out" — A blond
  husky Hal Chase–truck-
  ride to Raleigh, arr. 4:30

P.M. — hates South —
nothin to do, bars close
— New Caledonia, Louis
Transon, Noumea —
he said is Paradise —
— A bleakness I dont
like in air — dull
trees of Raleigh —
I feel forsaken —
    Old goodhearted taxi-
driver to corner — Curious
Raleigh Judge-type
    to corner —

Girls crossing — man
stops — Relief mgr
of restaurants —
Corn likker test, up
in Old Port — Mickey
Spillane, Faulkner —
Is going to rest finally at a
steady Maryland restaurant
— Then young kid in
old truck, married, who in
1946 hitched to Wash. State
with $500 & came back
with 21¢ — Then
incredible beat old car

with old fat bum, one
mile, incredible heat
   from motor, incredibly
dirty shirt — Then
2 bleak eternal bakery

workers driving home dogtired
from work thru red clay
cuts of Time, with wine
   faintly in gray western
   horizon, beefing about work
—I thought "Why do
you want men to be
better or different than
this" — One talked, other
didnt; one urged, other
brooded; left me off
at truckstop road to
Greensboro N.C.—broke
   $5 on coffee— "Dinning Room"
      Tics of Eternity
   called me buddy — good
hearted Charley Morrisettes
of Time—I must find
   langue for them—frazzly
   eager one & Charley Mew-
Leo Gorcey used-out legended

ripened-beyond sad fat one
— O Lord

    Great big G.J. burper picked
me up in the rain, dark —
after I talked to old bum
(70) in railroad hat who
said country was worse off
than in 1906 (truckdriver
from Liberty Tex. to
  Baton Rouge worried Mex,
  called it "tarpolian")
— GJ burper in new
huge Chrysler, was Chief
in Navy gun crews on Liber-
ties, also bought requisition
food (for Bainbridge Officers),
  at North River wholesale
  houses — ate 5 pound steak
    — ate 2 lobsters
at Old Union Oyster House,
    Boston — used to
  screw redhead at 7 PM
on her beauty parlor couch —
used to beat up queers in
Washington — Drove me
into bloody Western horizon
beyond rain (!) into the

glittering Lowell town of
Greensboro, gave me card
　　Robt J Simmons Lily
　　Cup Corp. — to Salvation
　　Army — was only gym,
old Negro born in Hollywood
("used to have a show
　on the corner with my
　sister & etc.") directed
me accurately "That
　Esso Sign, this side,
　　them <u>real</u> bright lights,
　　707 Bill<u>bro</u> St. —
　　bed & breakfast" —
　　Sho enuf — a little
　　ramshackle house —
dorm bedroom — man
was 50, thin, gray; <u>Red</u>
　got up in undershirt —
to talk about routes

("No sir, Winston Salem
　to Charleston waste your
　time, you in Charleston
　& Bluefield & you in the
　<u>mountains</u>" — hanging
　bulb, table, pictures of
　wanted criminals on

flowery wallpaper —
bathroom — "take
70 right on down the
river — ") Tennessee
River, from Knoxville to
Nashville — rain
starts — go to bed
at 9 — no eat — talk

with Red an hour about
rolling, wandering, sleep
  police stations, quit jobs,
drink whiskey, itch —
etc. — Dream all
night wild dreams of
big Chicago Salvation
  Army with wild young
  gang with me, & girl
horrors of my
wallet, Salvation Army
  underwear — incredulously
all over me I see six
inch long & thick sponges
  of fungus growing off
me — so awful I dont
believe it even in
  dream — spectral hap-
    penings, cellar, stairs,

rooms, bathroom, girl, boys,
wallet, (had it in my
pillow case so Red mightnt
steal it) — Up at 6:30
   "Gotta go" says boss
— breakfast: 2 coffees,
weak, cornflakes &
   evap. milk — & my banana
— & blowing drizzle out
but I go — & get spot
ride to junction — & get
  slow ride to High Point,
  dampwet, dry in car
  man was at New
  Zealand & Melbourne,
  — dry further in
  High Point Greek
  lunchcart with mottled
marble greasy counter

& aged grill & fry
smells & comfort, with
  steamy windows redglow
redbrick Hi Point but
   gotta <u>roll</u> —
(I got in that truck,
driver said "I'm quittin
  my job so the hell

with the insurance spot-
ters, less <u>roll</u>" —
bums in SA) — always
say, for truck driver,
<u>less</u> <u>roll</u> —
I got $4.85
Blank Universe stared
me on Main Hiway out of
Greensboro — storm rose —
driving wet drizzly winds —
I was positive I was lost —
faces of passing cars — Staring
porch people — bakery trucks —
but I got a spot ride
to junction — & there in
storm, got ride to High Point
— but woops, already wrote
this — Walked clear to
Furniture factories at junction,
& stood an hour 45 minutes, near
bleak aluminum warehouse
with tin chimnies with
Chinese hats, & smoke, &
Southern RR yards —
& funny Kellostone apt.
house with Italian in-porches
with potted palms, silent
& dismal & unfriendly

in the blank gray day—
Certain again I was
  lost—But—ride to

junction from a guy (I
  forget now!)—&
  there, on open hiway, I
  get ride from new car
    to Hickory N.C. <u>90</u>
  miles—with furniture
  veneer wood agent who
knows Yokleys of Mt. Airy
  & talked & was intelligent
(Sheepshead Bay, book review
for High Point etc.)—
at Hickory I was at
foot of my worse trip
—<u>mountains</u>—but had
no time to despair, a
  blond hero boy in a
  red rocket 88 ('52)
  with frizzly dog (half
  terryland Terrier & Sheep
  dog)—zoomed off to
    100 mile straightaway—
was only going to Kansas City
—1000 miles!—I
helped him drive—we

rolled thru Mountains fast,
thru Asheville (Tom Wolfe
sign on road) — (right
across Woodpen St.) —

to Knoxville, to Louisville
at midnight (pickt up
  lost hitch hiker in rain
  outside Mt Vernon, Ky.)
— but Oh those Cumberland
Mtns. from Lake City
& LaFollette Tenn. thru
Jellico to almost Corbin
Ky. — dismal, bleak,
I dreamed em, hillbilly
shacks, hairy buttes, smoke,
raw, fog — wow — at
Louisville the great Ohio,

the redbrick wholesale
bldgs., soft night, — cross
to New Albany, Ind.,
where I drove straight
across the Vincennes etc.
to St Louis in the morning —
he drove to Columbia
Mo. — I drove another 60 mi.
to Boonville — outside

Warrenton he wanted to
show — attendant —
ranout gas — on road —
went 117 M.P.H.!!!
Kansas City Kansas at
noon — I lost dark
glasses in his car — wild
kid — KC washed in
station, spent money
  on cokes & crackers
& ice cream — ride
  to junction — Two Texas

boys work in car shops
for Santa Fe RR in El
Paso drove me Topeka
— got there just as boys
were coming out of
work in Rocky Mt N C
car shops! — moving —
Then Beryl Schweitzer,
Negro All American back
from Kansas State, drove
me to Manhattan Kans.
— we talked — Then
two cowboys, the driver
14, drove to Riley
on Route 24 — talked

about horses, calves, roping,
drinking, girls, cross country
riding on "Satan" their
unshod bronc — etc. — with
  red hankies of cowboys
hanging on dashboard in
old rattly car — cowboy
  Sam called my seabag
  <u>war</u> <u>bag</u> — ! — at
  Riley I despaired, got
truck to junction — sun
going down — 2 boys
who come home from work
  drove me to Clay Center,
where I ate tuna in
backyard — & it got
  dark, I was souldead,
  I wanted to die —
so got poorboy port
wine, then $1.75 hotel
room with fan, sink —
right on tracks of R I R R
  or C B Q — slept 12
    hour log — washed, shaved,
  wrote, ate sardines —

500 miles to Denver, I
have $1.46 — but

feel alive again & even
that I will be saved, i.e.,
  I am <u>not</u> a dead duck,
<u>not</u> a criminal, a
  bum, an idiot, a fool
—but a great poet
& a good man—&
now that's settled I
will stop worrying about
  my <u>position</u>—&—concentrate
on working for stakes
on Sp. RR so I can go
  write in peace, get
  my innerworld lifework
    underway, Part II,
  for Doctor Sax was
  certainly part one!

<u>Clay Center</u> <u>Window</u>—
creamy snowy silo rising
Farmers Union CO-OP—
  green roof & old gables
  (once English style) of
  Clay Center RR depot—
  redbrick 1-story Plumbing &
  Electrical Co.—cars
  & small trucks parked
  on angle—rickety

brokendown shacks on tracks
—rickety graywood oldhouse
under noble trees, signs
on small barn, weeds, piles
of barrels or bldg. material
in back—someone is hammering
on a plank—W P Stark
Lumber Co. hugetruck backin
in a truckstop across the
tracks—fellow in blue
baseball hat in P&E doorway

is jacking up a car—man
in RR hat & man in Panama
talk & watch—sun's
coming out—US Royal
Farm Tires sign waves
in breeze—small Farmers
Co Op gas truck went
by—Tourists—Small
liquor store, was once gas
station, where I got wine,
white plaster, white fence,
green lawn, looks like
LA realty office—
music from a restaurant
juke—junkyard in dis-
tance—nobody on street

—everywhere the green
balls of trees over roofs
—last night a thousand
birds from the Plains were
yakking in this town—from
the Plains Clay Center is
a cozy nestled settlement
in the Huge—

It's the thought of Nin
that makes this trip so
sad—my sister didnt
love me, I didnt know
it—
The drink that's bitter
going down, & sweet in
memory—Life.
I am now stuck
outside Norton Kan.
with no prospect of
any ride, nightfall,
hunger, thirst, death.
Brierly saved my damned
useless life—I went
to Prairie View Kans. in a
truck, in a vale from be-
hind where I was, phoned
him collect, he's sending

—but why make a record,
he's saving me—he expects
to see me & be all excited
in talk & joy—like I
was—but am I dead?
—I want to say to him
"I dont understand what's
happening—any more—
I dont understand the
dew—I know there is
no Why but I cant help
it—" But he saved me
—I went from Clay
  Center in a car driven by
  blond handsome young
reclamation worker—we
  drove 60 miles west to
  Beloit—I felt very
  happy, the land of Kansas
    smiled—

days that start good end
up bad—at Beloit I
  got a ride from father &
  son (father road
  worker, apparently drove
  to Missouri to fetch him for
  holidays, is married to

'new wife') — to a
lone-ass junction at
281 — hot killing sun
— no cars — I thought
I was done for (was,
too) — I prayed to be
saved — a man carrying
a carseat load of dead
side beef (smell of
death) saved me —
my meaty dumb bones
— & carried me zipping
to Smith Center —

wrecked his car Feb. 29!
nice old fella — (on 28!)
    I know the joy those
little girls'll remember,
  in Prairie View with their
  mother — yes I do —
    And that cunt's tall
    grandfather — does
  my mother think I
    dont know those
      things? —
    Nobody cares —
    How can they care
  when they dont know?!

—At Smith Center a
  ride to a country junction
from a farmer hero
straight profile with
    little blond son—

  at ice cream stand, the
mother said to her son
"Dont hang around with
<u>him</u>" & I recognized her
face & she mine—mad—
but I got a ride to
(this was off Agra)—
  to doomed Phillipsburg
from carload of kids driv
by Marine ex & wife—
Okie—on I go with
dignified father & son
to that lonely hole
on a hill where I
think I die—2 hours,
no rides, zoom, sun
  going down, despair,
—Prairie View in
  truck—but later—

  I walked in with seabag—
Old falsefront western

wood stores, dirt, or tarred
  gravel sandy road Main
Street, cars crunch over
  majestically, on review on
  Sat. nites — but not a
  soul in sight, I'm going
  down over prairie hollow
  of trees bloodred, birds
    thrashing in trees, —
    I go to Public Telephone
    little old white house,
    woman long calls Neal
      for me (San Jose), he's
      not home — her husband
    in long overalls was
      once farmer, gives me
        hamburg sandwich huge,
        says (& also huge
        glass water) — "A man
dont know what to do
anyway." — Sun goes
down, I wait, — dark,
Prairie Viewers come round
for Satnite, men sit in
  front gen'l hardware, some
on ground, talk soft —
little kids hurry to
church suppers or whatever,

mothers — sodafountain
opens, I sit, watch happy
mother & little Gaby Nashua
joy girls — ate my heart —
  & crazy castrated lunatic
  Wellington chain smoking
  stuttering smelling somehow
  sweet & open air talks
    to me — Ah — "Born
    same date & year as
    A G Bell a great

intelligent" — "hmph,
a Swede, he's a Hollander,
there's Mr. So and so,
  barn burned down in '49"
    etc. — Pushes hat back,
wild hair brow pasted, mad,
somehow Fitz, I like
  him, he's <u>intelligent</u> —
"Kansas City was in
  street 2 nights — went
  to hotel — need 55¢
  says man — next night,
  need 75¢ says man —
  okay, — not got it —
  pushes me on left shoulder —
out" — "Dont work

any more since my
   headaches started" — "Old
   Mr Jones lived to be
   98 — died a
   mile north of that

water tower — couldnt climb
it tho, guess he was too
old — he was a Hollander
too" — Farmers: "Otto
is it? Hello Otto!" yells
Wellington — He's <u>sensitive</u>
— listens when you talk,
   jerks to hear & reply —
We cross street, longpants
   niceman driving to six
   miles east Norton — Mean-
while Old Justin's sending
me $12 Norton — goodbye
— they (longpants &
   thin heroboy of Kansas
   but sad & attentive) drive
   me to hill of Western Nite
— hail down stationwagon
   bein whaled at 85 by
   wild cunt — fixed me

a ride as only farmer
could — man in car
  says "Working late aint
  ya?" — (harvest he
  thinks) I get out
  car — "Thank you sir —
  and madame." Forced
    on them — Go to
    depot, agent off duty,
raging mad I tear up
  handful of folders &
  hurl them screaming
  across Rock Island tracks
    to where sad cows being
    waybilled to Santa Fe
moo — I go to Hotel
    Kent, get a room, promise
pay morning (first I
rush for wine, Gallo port)
— back — waterfountain,
  grocery store, man

wallet — hotel room hot
— windows — shower
no handles — curse —
dancing below — 5 shots
  wine — sleep — cold
  in Fall morn — up —

wipe wine from things—
depot—joy of
dark shadow morn on
RR tracks etc.—rush
to WU—back (water
fountain)—cash hotel—
Melroy Cafe huge
bkfast.—go—waitress—
read paper hurricane,
Faulkner crash airshow
"Please keep away—
for Gods sake keep
away"—bus at 5:30!
—I hitch!—
Cursing half hour, de-
ciding never to hitch
again, to end On The
Road (pure hitching)
with malediction gainst
America—a sunny
funeral director
from Hope Indiana with
particularly irrelevant
old bum carry me
80 mph. to <u>Denver</u>!
—"Believe in helping
out a feller—try to
do God's will as best

I can—" Never seen
a rattlesnake or
a mirage till this
ride! —Zoom—
Arrive Denever

ZAZA (Barbershop in Denver)

Zaza's—blue squares
painted above long
  vertical panes, on
  glass—says "Baths"
  & "1821"—Barber
    Shop—little tiny
    bulb light over door
    on protruding bar, bent—
    beat up doorway, gray
    paint below the mad
      cerulean wash blue
—in window burlesk
  ad, whitewashed flowerpot
of tub with soil & crazy
  redblossomed weeds—
    smaller pots, weeds—

no decoration, just bare
chip–painted weathered

old planks in window-
case, a can with soil
& greentip,—a milk
bottle, empty—a Wildroot
smileteeth ad card, a
   sad tablecloth over a
rail—an upsidedown
ancient piece of an ad
card—"Barber Shop"
is flaked half off—
Gaga's—other
window has ad cards,
same—Inside is wooden
      drawers, white—chairs
      white & black, old—
   cash register—barber
coat over chair—(closed)
—sink, bench—wood
   slat wall—calendar
—next to beat
Windsor shoe shop, used
shoes ranged in window

Late afternoon at the New
England Sunday lakes of
my infancy—
   The Joe Martin truckdrivers

of the <u>crosscountry</u> Denver
night — old lunchcarts —

Early Autumn in Kansas —
I ate a big breakfast of
sausages, eggs, pancakes,
  toast & 2 cups coffee —
hungry on the road — farmers
in the Sunday morning
cafe, the bright sun, the
  clarity of a rickety
  Kansas town alley out-
  side — heartbreaking
 reminders of Neal Cassa-
dy — "The Energies of
    Cody Pomeray"!

Alley: telephone poles,
wires, Firestone tire sign
(flamepink & blue), old
  graywood garage door,
  redbrick chimney lashed
  to a house with bar,
  aluminum warehouse, old
  streetlamp overhanging —
Norton, Kans. —
    Old shacks! — O
    America! — What was

it like in Lincoln's time!
　—Where are all the
railroad men of the
　19th Century! They've
all slanted into the
　ground—
　The heavy-headed
wheat—

ACROSS KANSAS

　Golden fields flaming
with the sunflower—
　Thirst-provoking-while-
chewing-gum mirages across
the dry plowed fields—
　but a dust-raising tractor
in the middle of a cool
　sweet lake is a blatant
　lie—"Many poor devils
died trying to reach one of
them"—(driver from Hope)
　　The immense dry farming
spaces—Majestical
white silo at Bird City
　Kans.—Distant
drunk phone poles—

      <u>A</u> <u>thirsty</u> <u>man</u> <u>looks</u>
      <u>for</u> <u>mirages</u>!

Colorado — old barn,
red — pile of dry boards,
barrels, tires, cartons —
dry wind, dry locust in
brown grass — old Model
T wreck truck — Wind
  sings sadly in its dash-
board — & thru wood
boards of floor — just wood
   slats for roof — incredible
   erect, skeletal — what
     deader than old car?
— haunted by old
  dead-now usages —
  rusty skinny clutch handle —
  no cap — drywood spokes —
  old ferruginous mudguards
I write on have tinny
  sad ring & sing while
   I write — pile of tarred

poles — Cows grazing
in the Plains haze —
  sweet long breeze —
  horse in the flat —

       prairie crickets tipping
—hay mtn. with
 old dead wagon 2
wheel—old dead
skeleton plows—wreckages
of old covered wagons are
 hinted at in the scattered
junk of backfield—a
  backyard to a barn
  & station that faces
  infinity—tremendous
  open dry white sand
  square to city, town—
  west of Idalia—

The Colorado Plains
horse neighing in immensity—
    Ah Neal—the shaggy
whiteface cows are
arranged in stooped
  dejected feed, necks
  bent, upon the earth
  that has a several
mood under several
  skies & openings—Ah
  the sad dry Land ground
  that's open between

grasses, whip't bald
by the endless Winds —
  the clouds are bunched
up on the Divide of
the horizon, are shining
  upon thy city — the
little fences are lonely —

The grassy soft face
of earth has pocks
of canyons, arroyos,
  has moles of sage,
  has decoration of
  aluminum wheat barns,
    the one skinny
    revolving windmill in
    the Vast, — lavender
    bodies of the distance
    where earth sighs to
    round — the clouds
of Colorado hang blank
  & beautiful upon the
          land divide —
the line of man's
land is the bleak
line of his Mortality —
  soft crunches the cow's

munch in all eternity
—shining cloud
worlds frowsily survey
the little farm in
 rolls immense of
  dun scarred breakless
grass—Sadly the
Continental Divide appears,
dark, gray, humped,
on the level horizon—
 The first crosser of these
E Colo. wilds first thot of
clouds mountainshaped—
 then—"Hey Paw I
 been lookin at them
  mountains for a hour"—
 "I have too, son—un-
 mistakably mtns.—not
 a cloud—" then the

party went into a long
 hollow—came up
 again on a rise—
(shaggy gray sensual
 cow lazing along)—
 but the rise not high
enough—for 5 hours—
:—"guess it <u>was</u> a mirage"

—Next day—
"Yes, a mirage"—
Vast earth flat with
  the blushes of the
  sun—of God—
  God is blushing on
the land—throwing his
    tints with a slant
    & sweep—& soft—
        "Yes, yes, yes, mtns!"
        "Unbroken miles of em!"

  Over the lavender
  land, snake humps—
rock humps—squat
  eternal seat forever—
  promise of raw fogs—
  (the beautiful hump
  necked pony, white &
  black, with Indian
  black strands personalizing
  his sweet neck & dark
  thoughtful eyes)—
  Vast eternal peak points
  there, shy to show their
  might till you come up
    close—Have deserts
    damned up behind em—

————clouds vie above
for mountainism—
they go darkening to
Wyoming territory North—
to Nebrasked dark gray
wall sky—cyclones
have formed there—
The sad mountains wait
forever—(heavy-bellied
pendant ringlet cow)—
(Madame Cow)————
The land of the Comanche!
I already smell that
Western Sea!—The
mountains (closer) are
misty, bright with
hazel, silver, gold,
territories of aerial
bright hover & bathe
them—Sad dry
river here, helping
out the So Platte—
thru the cities of

railroad & telephone poles
the mountains do cloud
darkly—Now I
see levels of them one

humping upon the other —
Smell the ozone & orgone
of the Plains where
the Mountains appear!
— the mystery of them
is like the gray sea —
because the flats rush
to meet them — &
traffics hasten seaward —
The pale gold grass of
afternoon, the cakes of
alfalfa, the hairheads
of green sage in the
brown plowed field, the
poles on the rim —
Snow on the mtns! —

Pure snow & tragedy of
Great Neal's home
town — Wild sweet
Mannerly of the Night
here rages rushing —
Tiers of mountains supra-
massing now — the Event!
Enormous golden rose
clouds far towards
Bailey, Sedalia, &
Fairplay — The

mountains loom higher
— Father, Father!! —
— Yes son, Yes son —
Lonely lost paths
lead to them over
rollhills of dark &
  pale land, Father —

Ah Son the silver
clouds above their
  Loom & Huge, the
  rains of them, the
  sad heaps of them, —
  The monstrous <u>block</u>
  they've made to our
  westward grand march
  — the flatland is
  here upchucked &
  rockened to hard —
  they swoop & slant,
  have sides — The clouds
  put on a splendorous
  air to oertop these
  Kings of Earth — the
  wind blows free on
    them from this
      lone prairie —

Estes has Showers of
light–mist — the
blue cracks to show
open heaven — the
Whole Plain descends
to be foothilled up —
yellow patches show
on those early sides —
beyond is black, &
wall drear, & Berthoud —
distant Pike the Giant
sleeps, black — his
shining snows now shrouded
in gales — Colo Spgs
rooftops are gray &
windswept now — but
Denver is snow, gold,
    sun, be–mountained,
        won. —

 Over the gold wheatflats
they rise blue as mysteries,
 sweet, dangerous —
   Oh Father the road is
 a thread to their knees!
Their mottled hills are
Indian Ponies! The
cornflower prairie is

their carpet of welcome
—Welcome to Bleak—
They are blank &
muscular rock upon
this naked earth—
this earth naked to the
blank sky, flat, oppo-
site—They oertop
our wagon tops & roof-
  tops now, & our trees—

  their smoky blue make
trees a proper green—
Stay so, tree— Ah
  the sad ass of my
  Palomino buttocking to
  the Great Divide—
In green clover hollows
  they fill the opening
  with their Merlin lump—
    Wild trailer cities
    on D's skirts!
      Old 1952! hallo!
        —Rockies? the
jigsaw fanciful cliffs
  of infant scrawls
  are no steeper!
  they have sides that

            sink like despair & rise
                        like hope —

with a still point
peak — Motels, Autels,
    Trailerlands! — they
    huddle on the Plain —
    The buildings & motels
    far out E Colfax are
    so new you couldnt
    smear shit on em,
    it would fall off!

        THE THING I LIKE ABOUT

Chinatowns, you look around,
you see that everybody has
a vice, <u>beautiful</u> vice —
whether it's O, or wine,
or Cunt, or whiskey —
    you don't feel so isolated
    from man as you do
    in AngloSaxon Broadways
    of Glare & Traffic where
    people might be hung up
    on shouting preachers, or
    lynching, or baseball,

or cars — Gad I hate
America with a passion-
ate intensity —

                    I'm going to excoriate
                    the cocksucker & save
                    my heroes from its doom.
                    It aint no atom
                      bomb will blow up
                      America, America
                      itself is a bomb
                      bound to go off
                      from within — What
                      monster lurks there, bald
                    head, fat, 55, young wife,
                    millions, Henry J Shmeiser,
                    out of his pissing cancerous
                    life will flow (from the
                    belly) a juice of ex-
                        plosions — dowagers
                          & young juicy cunts with
                          high mannered ways on
                          buses will gasp — I
                    stick my finger in the cunt.

America goes 'Blast' —
Fine people like Hinkle
  will be buried under the

stucco autel ruins — ah —
Lucien will rave —

> (Written when I was a railroad brakeman
> covered with soot mad as hell in 1952:
> I apologize now, America, in 1959, for
> such filthy bitterness but that's what
> I said then, and meant it.)

DENVER

The So. Platte at the
CBQ railyards — in
Sept. flows briskly from
the hump mountains
— sand island, — one sad
sunflower — weeds —
mudsides plopping off in
tide — water ripples
fast — banks steep,
  dumpy, reinforced with
rocks — pieces of tin
    strip, sticks, pipe —
    sewage pipes come out —
    oil rainbowing the water
    — many small beat

bridges — under the
RR bridge an old

concrete foundation, — oily
rocks — driftwood piled,
a-ripple — cans — dirty
pigeons — rock villages —
— on bank old dining
  car, red soot, for switchmen
— little trees growing
on the reinforced bank —
  but many tree stumps
  where trees cut — long
  islands of rocks —
  fast flows at sides —
  above this sad stream
  flowing thru iron tragedies
  are the brass clouds
  of solid Autumn —
Junk: - pile of tires, a child's
  crayon book, broken glass,
  coldwind, black burntout
  near sewage steam pipe —

        bolts, bird feathers, an
          old frying pan sitting in the
          crook of a bridge girder,
          old wire, flat rusty cans

no longer nameable, —
is written on viaduct concrete
wall: "If anybody were
in the Army in August
1942 when I shot
gent Slensa come
ant tell the Sgt."
(incoherent) — & drawing

in chalk of profile
with cloth cap, plaid,
top bop button, a
strange Skippy —
"All Judge
Suck Pussy"

Field of weeds, a plain
facing "The Centennial
School Supply Co." — "The
Mine & Smelter Supply
Co." — aluminum sooted
tanks — red tin sooted
sheds — boxcars —
concrete silos — redbrick
warehouses — chimneys —
& Denver skyline behind
not seen — in weeds is
piece of rope, piece

of car window stripping,
nameless rusty perforated
tinhunks, newspaper, old
    fold of handtowel
paper, old Jewel
      Salad Oil carton,

                a pile of junk, — & the
                girders of the viaduct have
                great black bolt heads
                  like knobs of a
                sweating steel black
                  city, — gray overcast
                clouds, cold — pipe
                of engine, steam hisses,
                cars skippitybumping
                overhead, clang bells,
                  iron wheel squeals,
                rumbles, — over the
                  silent mtns. a bird —

Near the Lee Soap
Co. is a collection of
ruined shacks — slivered
  burntout by time boards
    skewered, under the
      viaduct, cartons &

newspapers inside where
old boys slept — old
bottle Roma wine —
Old Purefoy Cassady
slept here — many
cans of many a
pork n beans supper —
strange festive weeds
with big cabbage
leaves & bunchy green
substance you could
roll into seeds between
palms — slivers of
wood cover ground —
old rusty nails long ago
hammered now lie
uppointed to heaven &
forgot —

A bum fire, sweet smoke
scent — Inside shack:
abandoned child toilet
seat! — Royal Riviera
Pears box — flashlite
battery — hole plugged
with cardboard but
boards spaced an inch —
The thrill of old maga-

zines time soaked — a
haunted village — wood
of crossbeam this door
is decayed where nails
went in, mould of dusts,
tiny webby darkgray
Colorado shack color,
a big old Rocky Mtn.
  tree overhangs — this
was once a thriving

                    Mexican or cowhand
                    camp settlement — mebbe
                    a big Mex family now
                      gone — Beautiful
                        lavender flowers 5 foot
                    hi in rich erotic weeds

— A redbrick shack
  with torn "Notice" —
  hints of onetime smiling
  people now the shithole
        beneath the
  viaduct of Iron America
  in which at last I
  am free to roam —
        Come on, boys!
      (Old Black Flag insect
      Spray! — for particular

      hobos! — but thrown
         from viaduct —)

   Deserted House — on
  tar road, many of
em — around back —
  great weeds — incredible
cellar stairs leading to
black unspeakable hole
  not for hobos but escaped
murderers! — Shit on
floors — papers, magazines
— Ah the poor sad
shoes of some thin
foot bum — weary
with time — scuffed,
browned, cracked, but
  good soles & heels only
a little edgeworn —
wine bottles — a
pocketbook "Trouble
  at Red Moon" —
Old newspaper with

faces of tragic Mexicans
in hospital beds of
the moment — now up-
stare this bleak roof

155

torn — old bum in
topcoat came in —
"Boys be around a
little later" — old
  Bull Durham pouches —
planks — trains go
  by outside — plaster —
  Boys who were coming were
2 Indians — one roundfaced,
  dungarees — one thin, tragic,
  seamed, Colorado Wild,
  with workpants, jacket,
red bandana & strange
rust red suede cowboy
  slope hat of the Wides
— coming across UP
  tracks with big bags

(of sandwiches probably)
— tied up with old white
bum who had strange high
voice, was Irish, old but
only 45, rednose, tremendously
hopeless, didnt talk to me,
went next room, read
  or scanned thru floor
  reading — what a movie
  of the Gray West I there

missed!—never felt the
thrill of the West
more since childhood days
of gray tumblewagon serials
in the Merrimac Theater
—cold, cold wind—
Wazee, Wynkoop, Blake,
Market—dismallest of
streets with RR track each
side, parked boxcars,
coldwinds blowing down
from all the gray Wyomings,

sheds with stairs, redbrick
bldgs., shacks, deserted—
poor little Neal in this
night!—and the alleys!
oertopped thickly with
telephone double pole
lines, barrels, concrete
paving, dismal, long, cold,
leading to gray Raw
each way—Then
Larimer, corner 19th,
Japs,—cluttered dark
pawnshops with tools,
guitars, lanterns, (some
unusable), rifles, knives,

stoves, bolts, anything
— & a poor Negro
couple quietly talking &
speculating as they walk in
to sell something, their
children will hear of it
   one day the down & out past

                        — beat Negros pile in
                        car, "see ya later," garage
                        Negro walks on, "Cool"
                        — but says <u>Cool</u> emphatically
                        & like a revolution —
                        Two itinerants standing
                        outside Pool Parlor still
                        closed 9 30 AM, every-
                        body cold —   Coffee
                        shop — cafe — next to
                        Windsor — old bum in
                          faded Mackinaw eating
                          big breakfast gravely
                        with grizzled sorrow —
                        younger men — coffee 5¢
                        — sugar & cream put in
                        for you etc. — Windsor
                        lobby cold, gloomy —
                        painting of constellation
                        of faces around Windsor,

                        Cody, Edwin Booth,
                            Lily Langtry, Baby Doe,

Oscar Wilde — Ah
this is all the Jack
London gray — Deep
dark stairways blood
mahogany — bums sit
   around — one man at
    bar — talk across 50
      foot lobby — once a
        great splendour is now
      mutter hall of hoboes
—clerk at sumptuous
  desk paces & whistles —
bums huddle in gray en-
  trance to smoke & see
  out, hands a pockets
—rattle rasp of
   a truck out there, I
   sense the gray cold
   tragedy of N's boyhood
—& its joy, too,
   as he showeth —

                    Bums sit forever, with
                    that hurt look, angry —
                    smoking — waiting — immov-

                          able from their position—
                          different type looks
                          out door humbly, waiting
                          for he knows not what,

—old tottering tall bum
in plaid shirt with
squinty look of bewilder-
ment—old painter
  bum in white coveralls
  struggles thru door—
  men with hats, coats, hands
a pockets, sauntering—some
  of em weatherbeaten, hard,
  rough looking, Canyon City
  was their most recent
      home—

                          Glenarm poolhall—
                          rubber floor full of
                          holes, boards show—ancient
                          lost linoleum under—
                          tables have hanging baskets
                            like balls—Pederson's—
                            old tin panel ceiling,
                            tan color—cue racks—
                            pissery in corner hid by
                            partition—greentop card

tables where Holmes
in bleak poolhall time
sat dealing blearfaced
& grim — "Onlooker's
bench" pale green, high,
sand jars — Candy
counter, open phone
booth panels, juke —
parkinglot across street —
Denver Bears on
summernight radio —

click, bounce balls on
hard, laughs, "God-damn!"
— husky voices — Stomp of
feet angling around ta-
bles — shuffle of shoes —
"Let's go, let's go!" —
voices of adolescents —
crash of break — "Shhhhhit"
— impatient knock of
cuestick on floor —
bop — click of ball
in basket — pocket —
Blackboard near counter
— groups of voices,
—

Street — Hotel DeWitt
— flash of liquor store
neons — Drake (blue)
hotel (red) down right,
cold — Bright orange
Chinese neons up left of
city center — Denver
Auto Park, lot, old redbrick
Hotel Southard one wall,
DeWitt (brownbrick white
bordered) other — over
head wire bulbs in lot —
Above poolhall Acme Hearing
Aid Co. whitewashed brick
— barber pole — (left)
Hotel Glenarm pink neon
on redbrick (right) —
Mirobar corner — (flashing) —

Counter — old bronze gilded
cash register — framed
licenses near coathanger
hooks — dark brown cabinet
— cigar counter with Tops,
White Owls, Red Dot — El
Producto — King Edward —
signs in entrance glass sides
low Coca Cola, Whistle

Oh Lord in heaven above
what a holy moment, coming
to Neal & Carolyn's house in
the gray fog day of San
 Jose, nobody in, the 9
 room sadhouse, the old
  Green Clunker filled with
  California Autumnal leaves
   like the prophetic old
   birdhouse wreck of old
    travels & sorrows — & finding
all alone in the house
Eternal house little John
blond & beautiful as an
  Angel, taking him up,
  a spot of Tokay, sit
 by the radio with him
  & have there on my
    lap all that's left
 of my life, as if he
were my blood son.

And he looks just like
  Carolyn — how sad
   the ten-balled years,
  how toppled the pin
 of myself — what
  Gray Sorrows of Autumn

for this sailing soul
—and for Cassadys,
nothing but love &
attention—bearded
doom boy Jack in Old
Jose, walked from
Easonburg Carolina—
with $5—& came
     to the Angel child that
     was not afraid of the
     Shroudy Stranger.

FRISCO Embarcadero Sept 8

Cold fog winds blowing
from the wreathed hills
of houses, I can see
the blazing fog shagging
over from old Potato Patch
in a cold whipped blue
—bay waters clear to
Oakland are ripple & keen
blue & cold looking—the
wind even whistles—The
majestic Mormacgulf with
her creamy white masts
 & rigging in the pure blue

          sits before me, a rusty
          redpaint waterline on
          the green Jack London
          swell of old piers —

   Cold wind brings hints of
all the good food in Frisco
(& maybe all the love,
 & surely all the hate) —
Mormacgulf is tied
with great cables, a
ratguard broke loose near
  the bowsprit canvas and
  bangs like a tin pan
in the wind — Water
rushes gushing from a low
scupper — In the water
is bread, a leaf of cabbage,
   a butt —

SP train at night

   The local — sweetsmelling
night soots — crashby
  dingdang of opposite
train — the pink neons
of Calif., the cocktail-

glass-&-mixer neon of
the ginmills — The hills
of supper lights — the
blear of fogs in from the
brown gaps — blear of
lights — Redwood City to
Atherton, clear, clean
night, with magic stars
riding the dark over the
homes of the railroad
earth — plenty time —
I must believe in the lives
of people & the history of
their reality — I must be-
come a historian —

observe the history of society
& write histories of the world
in wild hallucinated prose
— but a record of the
angels personalizing all the
haunted places I have
seen, written for the angels
not the publishers & readers
— a complete history of
my complete inner life,
also — Wail of the
train, chipachup of the

locomotive steams when
they open a vestibule door
— brakes haul up train,
old ornate browngreen coach
sways — Brown seats
of sticky stuff —
California Spanish neat
cut houses & Launderettes
& modernistic groceries
in the leafy black —

nameless newbrick mor-
tuaries or grass conservatories
or waterworks with
Shrouds — Oh old train,
Wail my Lowell back,
wail for my Lowell, make
my Lowell my only come-
back — Palo Alto, taxis
at bushéd sidewalk, lights
evenly pinpointing in a
main drag, — Dodge Plymouth
paleblue sign exactly the
one at Letran corner
in Mexcity — but with
beautiful bloodclot glow
Don Hampton beneath —
Strings of yellow bulbs

in car lot — A sudden
view of muddy wood
supports litup in the
construction night —

        Spectral palegreen <u>greenhouse</u>
         of a factory — Her
        I dont like & dont <u>have</u>
        to like & wont — Fuckups
        have a choice they make,
        in naked silence — I
        have never been a romantic
         lover like him because
        I do not like to moo &
        screw — I like straight
        relations no show all
         balls come & comfort —
          the slightest sadism makes
        me sicken — I am a
        hero — Distant bloodred
        antennas of Calif. —
         Murder will out among
         these beasts — that
         puffed feather She —

I like my women tragic,
silent, & ravenous souled
— Angel of Mercy,

come to swirl my brain
& teach me the truth &
what to do now, I pray
thee from dark & ignorance
—In darkness reeling I
see bare naked ledge of
oldbrown wood lit by
streetlamp, brown, dim—
Distant geometric modern
bluebright factory of
aircraft windows—The
star of my fame & pity
following far above—Lights
of spread parks illumina-
ting lonely bits of walks
—Green lights too—the

whistle calls on ahead—
Why did Sebastian live so
intensely & romantically
just to die blear-eyed—
he was saved from middleaged
baggy eyed ends—The
Old SP's all I got now,
Sam—I had loved you &
you me—Edie, I loved
you too, deeply—The
old stained glass of the

coach, the smoky tan
round ceiling, the barbershop
chairs, the engine calling
for our mountains & all
that's lost & was supposed
to happen & didnt—Ah
James Joyce, Proust,
Wolfe, Balzac—I'll
combine you in my forge—

Lovers like X. & Y.—simper
like snakes
WAITING FOR 146 AT
CALIF. AVE.
Backsteps Caboose (crummy)
bloodred—hills seaward
smoke shroud—sun orange
on its flare—Palo
Alto bank bldg.—steam
hiss, silence—the long
track Southeast—the
quiet Calif. cottages—
old paintchip trailer
in backyard, overturned
car junk, abandoned
cab (black, white), clothes-
lines with pins on—
Drive-In—Restaurant—

Green with modern ranch
  style redwood sections,
Swift's Ice Cream neon
  in window, big bamboo
  blinds in window, cars
parked around — Sunday
afternoon in San Jose,
  late sun, the haunted
  mountains from the East
  rim of Santa Clara
  Valley appear only after
  a second take look,
  dim, yellowish, faintly
rilled, round, bare as
  flesh, humping softly
  far over the flat of
  fruit trees — Beyond
   Drive In the night

                lights of a ballpark —
                traffic on road — Shadows
                of pretty girls passing
                inside Drive In — new
                cars everywhere, & lots
                 — lost spiritualities
                of America dulled &
                 buried in this last
                  barbaric land — empty

                    of meaning but rich,
                       fruitful, golden, — (the
                    land is) —
                          Original home of the
                       Tender Indian — the Pomo —
                       O Dostoevsky of
                       Indian Milleniums! —
                       Christian Fellaheen
                          Peotl Saint!

****

NOTES ON THE MILLENIUM OF THE HIP FELLAHEEN Oct. 1952, Calif.

With historical basis in this: -
(1) America is a pseudomorphological
     wave laid over the land
     of the culture-less Fellaheen
     New World Indian
(2) The American Race is
     West European, Faustian,
     Late Civilized, Decadent
(3) Faustian West will destroy
     itself; the New World
     Earth will return to its
     original Indian & Fellaheen

(4) The Indian is one with
the Fellaheen World Belt
thru Mexico, Africa, Aramea,
the Near East, Mohammedan
lands, India, China,
Korea, the Primitive
& the Fellah joined in
one Underground Mankind
  beneath Western & Russian
  Marxist heels — cultureless,
  non-critical, simplicity Mankind
(5) The prophet & saint of
the World Fellaheen Future
is a man of simplicity &
  kind heartedness & clarity;
  the various levels of the
  human godhead are
  defined in the separate
  religions which give decency

                    & richness in blank & blind
                    Eternity with everybody
                    waiting. Wm. Blake, &
                    Dostoevsky are of the same
                    Church! Jesus Christ & the
                    black Cunt are reconciled,
                    the Virgin Mary is painted

on the back of an immense
hardon of gesso plaster
in the hut home of my
Culiacan host, Mexico.

NOTE   (1) The Russian Christian
of the next 1000 years
belongs to the Aramaean
Springtime of the Soul

(2) The Aramaean Springtime
of the Soul coincides with
the Millenium of the
Hip Fellaheen which
has in it the seeds of
the Antichrist

(3) The next great con-
flict will be between
Hip & Christ, will be
resolved in the dark

———————
———————

——————

The Millenium of the Hip
Fellaheen has the subtle
AntiChrist in it—it
is not serious Finally—

Not Race, but the Types,
in Fellaheen Form, is
    Discernible; the slope
    shouldered cowboy switch
    man in dungarees, low
      rolled sleeves & brim
    hat is the same
    type as the samebuilt
    Indian driving a Mexico
      City bus or lost in end-
less meditation on the desert.

                    The types come & go &
                  never change, but history
                  changes; it is history
                    laid the pallor over the
                    face of same-built
                    Radio City executive — the
                    history of his Race. But
                    he who surmounts his race,
                    & sits beneath history, is
                      Fellaheen. Funny ideas.
                      The realization of the
                    death of a comrade is
                    Jesus; the Millenium
                    of Christ; the sur-
                    prised news of the death
                    of a comrade is Hip . . .

<u>Hip</u> is <u>Half.</u>
<u>Meek</u> is <u>Full</u>— or Whole

The Millenium of the Meek (Fellaheen)

Hip, & Culture, is Arrogance

Hip is the final Dionysian culture
  or cult-form in the decaying
  West Arm of Europe—
    it wears a subtle mask, it
    covers nothing.
     Fellaheen is Meek & Rages
    like a Beast—the faces
    of matricides in Athens
    or Cairo afternoon editions;
    over the hot rooftops a
    woman wails.
    The (Purely) Meek Shall
Inherit the Earth—the
  Children of God
  Children of Jesus
       of the Son of Man

        A mankind of saints shall
        occupy the final Earth,
        in endless contemplation of
        Heaven—

Hip Fellaheen will lead
to Meek Fellaheen, souls
sitting round a fire in
the open night
     All this (My Kingdom
is Not of This World) is
why 1947 was the
"happiest" year of
my life.
     Now no more tea,
but contemplation of
  Good & Evil—
  Lust & Sorrow

Burroughs the Boss of
the Jungle—
Carr the Boss of World
News—
  Ginsberg the trembling
Saint of the City—
   Cassady the worker
of the wheel on the
  land & cunt-man
    Kerouac the Pilgrim
of the Meek Fellaheen
     Huncke: - criminal hipster
     Joan Adams: - the Heroine
  of the Hip Generation

John Holmes: - the
Western "writer" &
"critic" — late Civilization
 anxieties & word-torrents —
Solomon: - Megalopolitan
            High Jew Enigma

                The Gospel of the Meek
                Fellaheen, Bringing History
                Round to Jesus, Begins in
                Sweet Actopan — &
                ends there

   I love the railroad
because it is laid out on the
 land, & requires the
  eyes of Indians — but
  the Rail is Evil
    "Brother have you seen
  starlight on the rails?"
    "Yes" —   but,
      the greatness of Wolfe
must have been in his
 realization of the land —

                Come face to face with
                the lonely grave now,
                beyond it is Heaven

                    —the lonely hole you'll
              lie in is the only hole
              you'll have—round it
              God has woven golden
              rewards the Fabric
              of His Glory—
              My father only now
          is blinking his eyes on
          the other side of Light—
                    Jesus loved the
                    Individual—
                         America is Decoration
                    now—planted palms in
                    San Jose—

The City fattens on
the blood of Towns,
then bursts. The
 Atom Bomb, or its
  satellite Power, will
  destroy New York City
  & all of Western Civiliza-
  tion from Marxist-
Faustian Vladivostok
westward round the
 globe to San Francisco.
  Then the Millenium
of the Hip Fellaheen

begins, in all lands.
But Eden Heaven
awaits the Milleniums
of the Meek Fellaheen
for all time
The Mankind of Saints,
that shall come after
& finally.
   The Men from Mars
are really the baldheaded
            bespectacled
   lobsters of American
   business. — really &
   seriously — their
   beady eyes, in fat,
   glint on the grave —

Rocky C.
A boxer with the
  sadness of a saint

Faustian society had
  good intentions

                 The latest sounds in
                 hip bop are exactly
                 like the latest develop-
                 ments in N.Y. Advertising
                 — the latest ad shows

an empty Coca Cola
bottle, a model with
a black patch over his
eye; these trivial things
are really milestones in
the History of Advertising
in Western Civilization, &
are momentous in the
concerned (Balzacian) circles;
in Eternity of the Meek
Fellaheen they have no
more meaning than that
a walnut fell on the
head of the Patriarch this
morning — or the

Messiah's pants fell off
the chair —

SKETCH

Crazy California of my
Selma days — tracks
of old SP shining in hot
birdy-tweeting breezy after-
noon, De Jesus & Rodriguez
market of white stucco

with cars parked (2) in
driveway & sign (same
   as above, over PAR-T-PAK
   board)—I see a
whole bookshelf of wine
      bottles, GALLO too—&
   here in field, in matted
brown grass under an
   avocado tree, I see

an empty Gallo Tokay
fifth & fillet of herring
can & beer cans showing
a royal feast of hoboes
in their California, &
bed-down grass of their
reclinations—In De
   Jesus (Vegetable, Meats)
I see a woman selecting
a brace of Cokes—a
   car parks—across road
is Ferry Morse Seed Co.,
all spectral iron hell
   red last night with
   browndeep clouds of
   locomotive steam in
Faustian sky—

A little strange SP
handtruck (handcar)

(in Kansas Rock Island
boys say "Nothin to
worry about but a nigger
on a handcar" — pricks)
goes by, with 5 Mex
Indians, one Negro —
they point to rails for
foreman Mex who has
sledgehammer — a Jet
screams above, from
Moffett Field — upper,
paler B-29 groans —
                — Seed
Co. is modern flat
plant, nobody in
sight, the machine
  silent in the red sun, —
At night not a
  human in sight,
just cars smooth in the
hiway, the rails gleaming,
cruel & cold to the touch,
  slightly sticky with
steel death, — lights of

airport pokers, distant
roar of Jets in wind
  tunnels, far off joints
slamming, planes carrying
Edison's light across the
stars & freights of
Machine Humanbeings—
& the block lights in
the night that give
  panic or peace
  according to the
   switch points as
manipulated—too
much iron, too much

                    for me—but in
                      afternoon, De Jesus &
                    the Tokay wine, the
                    roadbed rocks have little
                    silver gleams & waving
                    dry tendrils of interspersed
                    grass & crazy shuddering
                    little flowers & crackly
                    wind-weeds & pieces
                    of wood, hand towel
                    paper, cellophane
                      chip bags, gum wrapper,
                      little ants that bite—

           the juice of the grape
           stored darkly in the
            cool interior store, I'm
           wantin a poorboy—
            Beyond pink brick Seed
             Co. with its streamline

built in windows that
  hide controlled vibrating
horror (Rocky Mt. Mills)
is a field of fruit trees,
iron & barbwire fenced
from precious Company—
little white cottages of
the railroad earth, with
  end of day papa car
parked, little fruit
    trees—haze of
    sun—I'm sitting
    by silver painted SP

Telephone box & eq'pt—
wearing workshoes, asbes-
  tos gloves now black,
soiled timetable, thick
socks, ankle strap from
swollen ankle missing

                    bottom climb bar &
                    falling on rocks in
                    grim railroad dark —
                    blue work pants, too
                    tight, — gray workshirt,
                    — baseball hat for sun
                    — dreaming of my
                    $500 stake & Mexico
                    & the Millenium of the
                    Hip Fellaheen this winter
                    bla bla —
                            The Millenium of
                    the Meek Fellaheen

The intensity of D. H.
   Lawrence was not carnal

   A woman's cunt is
the soft avenue to her
womanhood, the godhead
of human generations,
     the yearning point
of man — I believe
the celibacy in the
teachings of Christ were
Paulist & Jewish-Castra-
   tion-Circumcision cult
   in origin — for if His

Kingdom is not of this
World, & the Soul is to
be Saved, it makes that
difference inside a
woman's legs when her
permission is given —

Neal's Pornographilia
is religiously intense —

The Phallic Cults
worship generation of
the species; the Aramaean
worships its Salvation

Jesus did not say,
but I believe in a
woman's permission

Retirement annuities
that grow out of group
life insurance & hospital
plans & sick benefits, spon-
sored by the modern big
company, are only an
attempt to cut out turn-
over of employees —
imagine devoting yr. entire

life, its soul & meaning
to a pineapple company
& accepting its retirement
annuities for reward —
"Stay with the Machine,
boys, dont need to run
away or shift to other
cogs, you're just as well
off in this one — we offer
YOU SECURITY TILL THE
GRAVE." — never mind
the Saviour, he never took
a shower. This company-
sponsored insurance, that
takes bites out of the
victims' pay all their
lives to support itself (the
money clangs hollowly
from the Machine's

twidget to the Machine's
twadget) is called
<u>protection</u> — protection
against their being left
to drift free outside the M.
(M. for machine).
   Big Business in Late
America prides itself on

growing figures, just as
a spokesman for the
Golden Age, "the American
Explosion," points with
pride at the 3 inches
added height average of
  American kids.
    If not the highest,
then it's the "fourth
highest" etc.

  The faces & demeanors of
successful young American
businessmen: - a guarded
sense of one's own
  gentlemanness — the
  face taut & ready to
  smile the hand-shake
  smile — a terrible
concern in the expression
  that the subject wont
  reciprocate the same
  escalator tension from
  empty gesture to empty
gesture — these gestures
are the ritual of Late
High Civilization — the
  American workingmen

have adopted a surl
in superficial opposition —
　　but the Executive

　　　　　　　　　　　secretly & queerly desires
　　　　　　　　　　　　the Worker's "tough look"
　　　　　　　　　　　　& the Worker (excuse me,
　　　　　　　　　　　　the Man of Production
　　　　　　　　　　　　in New Overalls) secretly
　　　　　　　　　　　　practises Executive Smooth-
　　　　　　　　　　　　ness before his mirror.
　　　　　　　　　　　　　　Ad infinitum —
　　　　　　　　　　　　　　First signs of the
　　　　　　　　　　　　Machine really destroying
　　　　　　　　　　　　itself & People is the
　　　　　　　　　　　　guided drone plane with
　　　　　　　　　　　　Atom Bomb warhead
　　　　　　　　　　　　— "DRONE" is the
　　　　　　　　　　　horror name, deeply
　　　　　　　　　　　named by mysterious
　　　　　　　　　　　High Priests in the Forums
　　　　　　　　　　　of the Pentagon Glare.
　　　　　　　　　　　. . (I worked on the Pentagon)

　　The gray drab Indian
village near Actopan, no
　　Coca Cola, no Orange Crush,
　　just dysentery-ridden

water, & lizards on the
old walls — Jesus has
made it hard on us.

But a maiden wears
a smile, & a little
  hidden ribbon of meaning,
& at the brook the
waters ripple in the
  shade of shepherd
  trees — the flies are
insistent, but so is the
  soul in its thoughts &
  loves, O Man, Poor Man
— Thirsts developed in us by
the Machine are insatiable

As for "freedom" —
there's no doubt of
freedom in Fellaheen

Cathy says: "Write it
right here now."
    "Look at her legs
move" (the bug) "she
wants to eat."
    J: Nobody eat the
bug.

C.: The bug eats the
shades up.
       J.: I bounce (bowtz)
Pee pit (paper)
       We baint (paint)

That paused look of a
man pissing—

"Silly Faust—& the
mystery of history"

 J: Arent you dired?
C: It's a nightgown—

The Agrarian American
is the strongest American
because nearest to Fella-
heen condition

<u>Santa Barbara</u>
(1) New notebook
(2) Spoon
(3) Toothbrush
(4) Lunch
(5) Dostoevsky
(6) Matches for lamps

The Fellaheen women
let the men run things
—in the driveway of
the country store on
  Sunday afternoon, they
wait in the car & smile
while the men goof with
  beer cans—These are
  Mexicans, Indians, of the
   California countryside—
Western Civilization women
would say "Are you
    <u>coming</u> John?"

                    American woman run
                    things, even kicks,—
                    have made life a drab &
                    sorrowful for their
                     Milquetoast Machine
                     husbands, the dumb fucks—
                      also the American women
                      have subordinated everything
                      to "my child"—my
                      so-called child—(the child
                      of God, lady)—& so
                      make the husbands attend
                       to the children only—
                       Fellaheen children are in

the background silent,
watchful, & awed —
American kids are loud,
nasty, forward, disagreeable
at 4, & bored at 16

The horrible bitches have
no regard for man
anyway, just their
itchy old twats & what's
  come out of it — It
would never occur to
American women &
American Old Woman
Society that a 80
year old man's life
is more valuable than
an infant's life because
it has acquired its
value — They think
in terms of "My Child"
with an almost-mystical
sense of the Future
as abstract as every-
thing else Faustian —

A jet plane is an
abstraction because it

serves absolutely no
 purpose to body or
  soul — just flies —
        All their other ab-
stractions — Communism,
Freedom, etc. — are
abstractions within the
Abstract Structure of the Machine —
Machines can't
run without a theo-
retical basis.
        The theoretical of
 Nature is still & will
  always be "unknown"
because it is not
 theoretical, it <u>is</u> —

                    Ah now the croaking
                    birds of California Aft-
                    ernoon, the tweeties too,
                     the neigh of a horse,
                     the breeze, the rustle
                     of a paper bag stuck
                      against a bush — God
                     will come again in all
                     his radiance & illuminate
                    our souls with understanding
                     & pity, & Jesus will

descend into our minds
with his Meek & Sorrowful
Look & pierce us with
the pang & arrow of
   our condition on the
   plain of life—& bless
   us with a soft
      shroud—I want
      to sit in the

desert contemplating the
   earth & the clouds &
   the insects & suddenly
   the poor Fellaheen
      simplicity-souls there
   with me—I want to
   be among them in the
   night, soft lights across
   the sand road, distant
   dogs of the Fellaheen Moon

—the maguey rows—
the holy marijuana to
   enliven my Vision when
   needed—the sweet
   wine—to soften my
      cark & belly when needed
—the tender cunt of

my Indian Love — my
   Fellaheen Wife — &
      holy sleep among the Patriarchs

                              All I want to do is
                              love —
                                 God will come into
                              me like a golden
                                 light & make areas
                                 of washing gold above
                                 my eyes, & penetrate
                                 my sleep with His Balm
                                 — Jesus, his Son, is in
                                 my Heart constantly.
                                    My brother Gerard
                              was like Jesus. My
                                 father I loved like
                                 God. My mother
                              is sweet & golden-
                                 hearted & never meant
                                 harm to bird, insect
                                 or person in the depths
                                 of her simple heart, —

My sister is dead to God
   now, because she puts
   marriage to a tyrannical
   but simple-hearted

man before her knowledges
of God & the soul that
  she learned once from
  her father, brother (&
  mother perhaps) & Church—
    She & I knelt in
  damp pews of poor Good
  Friday—
    I am working for the
  railroad to keep my
  stomach in food &
  drink but I want to
  throw myself on the
    ground & die for God
    if it wasnt so awful

TO DIE & leave the joys
of food & drink & cunt,
  & grieving relatives.
    To learn the life
  of sainthood is harder
  than 8 years of
  Medical or Law School
  —I will come to it
    gradually, to celibacy
  & some fasting (by celibacy
  I mean of course simplicity
  of living, for instance no

gum chewing & such
  trivial habits that attach
to me still from the
Machine of Anti Christ)
—come gradually to growing
 my own food, to Patriarchy
  & Silence in the Earth
   & Ecstasy of Alyosha

SKETCHES NO. 3

  Cowboys of the Wild
American romantic West
  & the Horsey Set are
hungup on horses' asses —

        Cows around an oil well pump
            say — "Leave the oil in
            our earth." — Later ages
            will wonder why Faustian
            man extracted all kinds
          of stuff from the earth,
            dirt, mud, oil — Silly
            pumps ass balling up &
            down the ground for
            nothing — oil for horror —

(—Dostoevsky's moon—)

Aping nature is not art,
only a gospel will do—

Tea—backtracking thru
the universe—

Not only a derangement
of the senses but of
personal evaluations, moral
evaluations of yourself
—tea is suicidal—

I vant to be alone—
since that repudiation of
a human wish Americans
have become adjusted to
their machines—

—

Baby crying in gray morning
—moments meshing with
every note—

Pray to God for the
great reality (on
yr. knees in Italian

railyards near spectral
    tenements)

  The first thing that strikes
me about Dostoevsky in begin-
ning any of his books is
the nervous anguish that
  seems to have preceded the
first page — the hero is
always the same, comes
  to the first page out of
    eternities of introspection,
    anguish, gloom — just
    as I do every day.
      Hmm.

The morning of me
liberation — Oct. 4, 1952
— I go live alone in
a 3rd St. room, leaving
Neal's — for the 1st
  time since 1942 —
(in Hartford) — All
  set to write <u>On</u> <u>the</u>
  <u>Road</u>, the big one
  with Michael Levesque
— the only one —
  have renounced everyone,

& myself dedicate to
    sorrow, work, silence,
    solitude, deep joys of
    the early mist —

Train 3-419 is waiting
outside Oakland yards
— it's 7 30 AM —
fog — great clutter of
bedsprings & screens &
rusty fenders for walls
make a house of
ferruginous barrels loaded
with iron mucks — I
see whole interiors of
hotplates, grates of
old stoves, the arms
  of antique washing ma-
chines, tubes, buckets,
— two bos just
  passed it, found an
    interest in a piece on the
    ground — Strange
    bird flies overhead —
    Saw 1000 ducks Milpitas —

  Next to junk crib
is concrete blockhouse hut
with protruderant pole

with climbing ladder &
iron pipe—a smaller,
  sloperoofed concrete house
  with no meaning (hides
  a dynamo?)—little
window—in chalk
  "Nixon is broke"—
Armour & Co. loading
platform has yesterday's
  debris—a Filipino
fishes in blue barrel—
  October & the railyards
again, & the great novel
  in America—
    The Cook is Grooking—
    Jacky Robinson's at
    bat again—

                    OCT 4

          Saturday morning in a Frisco
          bar, October, it's the
          World Series as in 1947
          when Michael LeVesque
          was in Selma Calif.
            & the old railroad clerk
          spoke to him in the

                              203

long dust of an
afternoon of sorrowful
farewell, when Mike'd
turned for one last goodbye
at Teresa in the
long grape row—

I'm getting my kicks in
  typical Jack Kerouac
way, refilling a tokay
25¢ shotglass from
my poorboy pocket bottle
in railroad-grime jacket

& writing & watching
W. S. while Negro &
Filipino cats sit in
bar watching game
without buying or
  drinking anything at
  all—Mike Levesque
is like that, the
  Pilgrim of the Fellaheen
is a simple & joyful
  fellow & no "innocent
boy" camper like Peter
Martin—but no

more words, now for
    the scenes —
        (She was born in Montreal
    a simple-intentioned pure
        heart, & remained so for
        a lifetime thru histories, paranoias
                        & grief)

  You've got to put a
superstructure of love
on yr. life or you'll
just be a skeleton in
  the grave of yr.
mortal days, shuddering
naked against the main
  nerve of yr. being,
unclothed for the
  Raiment Halls of
  Will, Severity of Purpose,
— God is a superaddition
  to the frame of Man,
like the flesh & eyes —
Therefore unravel the
drama of yr. soul before
yr. eyes, be strong &
thoughtful, be not naked scared

The personal legend of
Duluoz is for communica-
tion on a later level—

When I walked in 20th Century Fox
office in 1949 I knew the
corruption of certain types &
the City; but now I see the
corruption of all America
& its broken head on an iron wheel

Ah what's happening in
the world!—

I woke up—2 flies
were fucking on my forehead

———

———

—

It's hypocrisy makes
these hills grim—

The <u>pue</u> of the sad Malley—
listen to the sad Malley—
the <u>phew</u> of the sad Malley—
song of the sad Malley—
            (Mallet locomotive)

—

You have an inordinary
nack to inult me
every nime
        This is the end of
the handball game
        TO CARL SOLOBONE

SKETCH . . . .

Watsonville, valley — the
sun is setting in a mysterious
orange flameball over the
flat green lettuce fields
interlined with brown dirt
  rows & roads & rails — beyond
   the milky haze of this
   dusk is the sea, unseen, the
   Pacific to the Land of the
    Rising Sun — the grass is
   like hay, full of ants
that go to sleep at sundown,
   dry shrubs, dry cottonwoods,
weeds, tart spice ferns of
  Spring are now fuel for
    Autumn Seres, — little
  weedflowers close their
    blossoms as the dusk birdsongs

titter — a farm in the
dreaming vale below, white-
washed barn, flat reposant
chickencoops & toolsheds —
  I hear the distant hiway
    trucks — sitting on the
  mat of earth on the west-
  ernmost American hill facing
  the unknown east all
pink now — Sweet dewy
  breeze hints of sea —
The railroad cries the
roundroll — I sleep on
the ground under the
stars like an Indian,
  baseball hat, brakeman's
  lantern & tucked in
  Levis & workshoes &
  jacket, arms folded to
    the moon —

                    a cow mourns below —
                    adios — now the sun
                is bloodred, sinks behind
                  the mighty mountain trees
                  — the distant sad hiway
                  of little soundless cars —
                  the Salad Bowl of the
                  World sinks to dark, all

you need is a plane to
spray mayonnaise & chopped
scallions — eat a whole
valley raw — the figs
 trees are shitting on the
 ground, Mexican Motorists
 pick walnuts from the
  ground, the bums have
  left a Tokay empty
 under the avocado tree —
  ripe California

THE CRUMMY

Where once I'd quake
at the thought of a
 jawbreaking caboose hitting
in the slack, Wham! —
 now, this morning, in
 my bemused equicenter
I look up & see the
 caboose crazy disheveled
blurred, as if I was seeing
 it momentarily photographed
 thru a trick mirror, &
feel no shock or wonder
nor hear a sound nor

move from my seat—
   just <u>see</u> it as it
   rocks to the bang

                    Now that I understand
                    the railroad with my own
                    senses I see that Neal
                    was only jabbering about
                     the obvious again, & in his
                     unnecessarily involved &
                       confusing way—which has
                       to do with his sadism—
                       to <u>confuse</u>—unclear
                       & befrought with subtle
                       "lies" or "hiddens"—
                       "hidings"—concealings—
                       —from weird guilt—

                    The Bird of Chittenden

OBRA PRIVATA
   When you were a kid,
Duluoz, & the perfumed
   aunts visiting & the
promise of quarters &
   ice cream & lipstick
     kisses & long afternoons
   of gossip in the kitchen

as the sun gets red—
The Immortality &
Eternalness of all
that & everything that
ever happened to you
still waits for
that Obra Privata
pen, sorrow & faith—
(some of it in French!)

MORE SKETCHES CALIFORNIA

Sexy young Wop mother
waiting train at Burlingame
in Gray West Void with
blond son, campy meets
her brunette sister in a
suit—a semi wino in
brown & white saddles &
beat pants passes them
smoking with that "Hey
Jack, I'm tired & shore
weary" expression—Big

sad baggage boy pushes
trunks on orange truck,
crepesoles, buttondown sweater,

short hair, his mother's
making chocolate pudding
for him right now, his Pa's
   puttering in the garage—

                    Hundreds of cars parked
                    in concrete back of
                    Bridge & Dugan Carpet
                     Specialists—A big
                      yellow squash in the
                    weeds near the railroad
                    fence of a California
                       bungalow settlement
                    with same backs—
                    Pale green dobe oil
                    company buildings—
                    (ranch style)—
                      Bay Meadows, the
                    starting gate high
                    on the far turn above
                       the immense Bay
                        flats & wreckage
                         of cranes & poles—
                    blah—The Machine Plain—

   The California Okie
businessman with bushy
eyebrows & red face

clumpin along adjusting
his belt butt in mouth
newspapers sticking out
of shroud coat, in
first rain of year —
in Hillsdale — thousands
of cars everywhere half
of them new (now's
time to buy jalopy)
    Brown-grass hills, green
redwoods, alpine lodge
houses of 30's Calif. —
Gray murk on palms —
Western Awning Co.
    palegreen stucco —

                    & <u>Dentist</u> in Spanish
                style — Dullness of
                Texaco station, "Marfak
                    Lubrication" "Motor Tune
                    Up" — attendant pissing
                    water on windshield —

— Rain on the
parched Calif. brown
    grass hills — the sea
    beyond — Ha! —
What will be debris

by Europe track? —
   here is oil cans, beer
   cans, paper (brown),
   oiled tie-piles, boards,
   cartons, lumberyards,
    junkyards, cellophane —

               The winter in Italy? —
               April in Paris! —
                 January in Venice! —
                 Summer in England
                 & Scandinavia!
                 Fall in North Africa!
                 Winter in Baghdad!
                 —!! —

CONSUMER CREDIT &
  the new E. A. Mattison
  Budget Finance Plan
  Inc. is just a loan
  to someone to finance,
manufacture, distribute &
  sell a product, such as
  home freezers — But this is
going in debt in order
to pay it off with
savings. You borrow
money, buy or invest, &

then save to pay off your
debt: leaves U.S. with
record savings & record
debts at same time.
Consumer credit is one
arm of machine reaching
out to help other, but
under conditions of debt.

In other words, <u>Debt</u>
(Neal's big hassle) is the
form, financially, the Machine
creates to <u>enslave</u> the
individual to <u>It</u> — for
instance, Sinatra owes taxes,
back taxes, & is "forbidden"
to go to Europe, also
Dick Haymes — The
collusion of Debt, the
"Tax," & "Insurance"
are tying people closer

& closer to the great
Wheel Rack —
Don't accept "Loan"
or "Arm" of Machine —
it is a deceptive enslave-
ment — simple souls mis-

trust offers of loan for no
          idle reason —

                    The traffic problem is
          merely that cars by the
          millions enslave us to
          new city systems requiring
          hours of driving to & from
           needs, on "congested" arteries,
          naturally — where once
          you'd-a walked — These
           are all conditions pointing
           to the imminent cancerous
           death of America, the
           Final Cog in the Western
           Civ. Machine — the
             supreme end-result of
             early Gothic Phallic forms
             is the skyscraper & the
             oil drill & powered
             compressor & pistons of
             great engines — the Machine
             copulates, men aren't
               allowed to any more —

  The flesh gets numb,
but the soul doesn't.

N's feeling for "Marylou" in
  that pix — her sexual
  pinched pretty face — he
    doesnt realize about flesh
  is numb — till she'd die,
    I say — Candlelight in
    a beat room

                    The rat of hunger
                    eats at your belly,
                    then dies &'s left
                    to bloat there —

WATSONVILLE GRAYMORN,
  a barbershop near park
is doing big business at 9:45
    AM — gray overcast, raw,
    cool — The park grass
    clip't to the sward — a
    thin grayhaired fastwalking
    lady in low heels hustling
      towards Main St. of 5&10's
(Woolworths), "City Drug
    Store," Ladies Shoes,
    Stoesser 335 Building,
    with Physician X Ray
    Doctor windows above, &
    "Roberts" Just Nice Things

(Store) — In the barber
shop a Brierly-like barber
in neat glasses & white frock
lowers little boy from

littleboy chair — Name
of shop is "Virg's" —
with an Anson Weeks
band ad in glittering win-
dow & a few bottles of
hair lotion — Little boy
was with mother who
trots him pushing him
along across park in her
big ass gray slacks, ban-
dana & crepesoles —
little boy has wool cap
over new hair cut —
Trucks of supermarkets
& Oakland Towel Co.
& just pickups without
lettering grumble around
park — The palms
hang dull in bleak

green bug-specked Void
— California on a
gray day is like being

in a disagreeable room —
  Here is lineup around
  barbershop: "Sodas
    Shakes Sundaes" in old
    fashioned Watsonville
    sidewalk roof corner but
  not Western; solid &
    Victorian, once respectably
    whitewashed, with <u>bas</u>
    <u>relief</u> drape regalcords

  & a "Surgeon" goldpaint
  flecking off a round
    baywindow — "Athletic
    Supplies" — Sharp's Sporting
  Goods next in same bldg.
    — fancy fishingpoles

                in rich interior basketball
                gloom — then "Ben's
                  Shoe Service" not cluttered
                but prosperous & shiny like
                he sold shoes — then
                  the old arched wood
                  doorway of old bldg. with
                  <u>bas</u> <u>relief</u> sprigs — & a
                  doctor plate — Then
                    Steve's Cocktail Bar,

shuttered with French
blinds, black tile base
of wall, cocktail glass
drawn under "Steve's"
— Then City Club
restaurant, same shuttered,
but open door, red "Beer"
neon — (bells ring now)
— (for Ten) —

Then barbershop; then
"Smoke House," an
ordinary cigar newspaper
store — "Pajaro Valley
Hardware" sandwiches
in old Colonial Hotel
bottom of 2 story of
which is Sporting Goods
— Then rich creamy
concrete streamlined
bank on corner, with
official Main St. globe-
type (5 globes) streetlamp
announcing bleak official
clock district officer
corner of bus stops
traffic & stainglass
doors

In Pavia, 18 miles south
of Milan, the ashes of
St. Augustine, the great
monastery Certosa di
  Pavia, junction of the
    Ticino & the Po, fortifica-
    tions of Old Ticinum,
    thousand yr. old university,
    manufacture of pipe
    organs, makers of wine,
    silk, oil, and cheese.
      <u>Must go to Pavia</u>

 Taranto for oysters

San Remo for swimming

Padua for pictures

Stone Age village near Terni

<u>It</u> <u>not</u> <u>to</u> <u>pay</u> <u>is</u> <u>not</u>
<u>a</u> <u>sin</u> <u>to</u> <u>Jesus</u>

ON THE ROAD
            BY
Jack Iroquois

Billy Caughnawaga

The "angelic" light
 behind Joan in that
 "radiant angel Mary"
  dream — if so, Edison
  is God because it's the
  electric light gives her
  her glow — Only in America
   a woman is condoned for
   putting the man out of the house

Half of mankind is
    Snakelike

Ah Duluoz, — when you
   left home to go to
  sea in 1942 — that
  was the beginning — then
  you'd sing <u>Old Black Magic</u>
  in the night, & love
  yr. thoughts, & Margaret,
  & yr. good little friends of
  Lowell — Sammy GJ
  Salvey Scotty Daston
    —

— what have you
gotten since? Edie in

the Fall led to Joan
Adams Summer 43,
which led to Carr,

> Burroughs, Ginsberg, Chase,
> which led to Neal —
> & Tea — What would
> you have if you hadnt
> written Town & City? —
> NOTHING — At least you
> met Holmes, especially
> Ed, & Tommy (they'll al-
> ways be yr. friends) —
> & now you know that you
> must depend on yr. self,
> & love the few who love
> you, & try a disinterested
> love of even yr. enemies,
> but must work like
> Joyce now, "silence,
> exile, & cunning" —
> All on your own
> terms, in yr own intelligence

—Never mind what
Burroughs, or Ginsberg, have
to say about anything
—start by exposing them

all in your parable a-
bout America: -
 THE MILLENIUM
 OF THE MEEK FELLAHEEN

Then work on "Vanity
of Duluoz" with
original ms. & all
new Duluoz memories —
in Mexico or in Spain —
in Paris or in Pavia —
Fish out that old
 "Liverpool Testament" —

    concerning Duluoz —
    For now — we'll start
    (& remember yr FrenchCanadian
    soul) — <u>Compren</u> <u>tu</u>?
    Bon — commence —
       Oct 28 '52

The old cowboys of
1930's pulp westerns were
always in river bottoms
eavesdropping on the rustlers
at late afternoon — the
Pajaro River in dry
California, brush, sand,
cow turds, trees —

ashes of old campfires —
Nowadays the wino

                    there realizes the old cow-
                      boy must have had that
                      canteen of tequila forever
                      upended, the way things
                      are — Peeking thru
                        the brush at the doings
                        of other wino-rustlers
                        jacking off or cooking
                          pork & beans makes you
                          realize once & for all
                          the world is real &
                          pulp & pocketbook B
                          Movie magazines are
                          unreal — the late sun
                          on the cattle tracks, the
                            flies, the sad western
                            blue —

    The flame of the
woodfire grows more profound
& mellow on the first
  November nights, in
          the caboose —

                    Remember that picture of
                    Edw. G. Robinson, a Bowery

bum drunk, visiting a
Class Reunion — saw it
with Pa — it's as though
I, of the Pajaro Riverbottoms,
should attend the Columbia
    Lou Little Reunion of
$6 a head & $4 for
    game tickets — in
    poor Halloween! —
    Oh Soul —

    "The trouble with me is that
    outside my mind it seems
    the world hasn't got no
    ass," speech to Alumni,
    Dostoeyevskyan, embarrassing,
    significant

MANTELES PARA LA MESA

  The poor little Mexican
gal in Calexico, writing
on Oct 1 1952 to Manuel
Perez in Watsonville whose
clothes & belongings I found
intact on the Pajaro levee
dump, wants money to

buy a <u>tablecloth</u> — can
you picture an American
woman asking money for
such a humble, useful
purpose — "unos manteles
para la mesa." "Honey,"
  she says, "dime porque no
  me has escrito" — "tiene
  tan . . . pensamientos para ti."
    She loves him — I am
    wearing all his clothes not
    knowing whether he's alive or

                    dead - or in the Army?
                    I found several of her
                    sad letters on that dump,
                    in October, — in the dry
                    dust, just before the rainy
                    Season, —

                    Me: a man made to
                    stand before God —

          Who is the Montgomery
          Clift Stanford kid
          reading Shakespeare in
          the 12:30 local on
            Oct 31 AM 1952

—what ignu? what
sonnets of his own?
does he realize Kerouac
is writing the Millenium
next to him, in workclothes?

OCT 31 1952

Evil dies, but good
 lives forever—
   The evil in you will die,
& your flesh with it, but
the good in yr heart &
 soul will live forever—
   Evil can't live, good
can't die—

   Your angrinesses, impatience,
hassels, even that & your
shit, all—will die, cannot,
wills not to live; but the
 flashes of sweet light will
 never die, the love, the
 kindness of hope, the
  true work, joy of belief—

            As for reforming others,
            let them reform themselves,
            if they can't they were

meant to die; they
are barely alive now if they
can't reform themselves to-
morrow; better a cleaner
of cesspools than a re-
former. Let <u>every</u> <u>man</u>
<u>make</u> <u>himself</u> <u>pure</u> <u>as</u>
<u>I</u> <u>have</u> <u>done</u> — that's
the "reform" —
    Work on your own soul —
experiment to see if one
man can be saved, as
the whole lot en masse
  can apparently not —
    on yr own soul first,

then the angels of
your soul, yr mother, your
wife (a new, good wife),
your children. If a son
or a daughter is bad,
throw it in the sea —
  Your few good friends.
  Cultivate yourself like a
  flower; pull out weeds
   like Cassady, Ginsberg,
  Burroughs; accept the
  nourishment of White,

Holmes:—water yrself
carefully—& keep your
flesh fit so as not to
burden the soul with
temporal strains & remove
    that much energy

                    for its prime considera-
                    tion & meditation—
                        God, & Good—Direct

contact between you &
  God means no church,
  no society, no reform,
  & almost no relationships,
  & almost no hope in
  relationships—but
  kindness of hope inherent
    in that what is good,
      shall live, & what is
        bad, dies—Your
      flesh will be a husk,
        but yr. soul a star—
            The greatest & only
      final form of "good"
        is human—

                    Because intellectual
                    & intellectually willed

good & so conceptual
good is only a word —
"Almost" no hope in
relationships, means,
no foolish hope, but
true hope —
Everyone to his own
<u>true</u> <u>work</u> — There
is no good in work
which does no good.
Railroads, factories,
solve & give nobody
nothing, serve the
flesh only, at great
time & sacrifice, are
evil —

The true work is on
belief; true belief
in immortal good;
the continual human
struggle against
linguistic religious
abstraction; recognition
of the soul beneath
everything, & humor, —
Lights in the foggy
night are not necessarily

bleak & friendless, but
just lights (in fact to
light yr. way), & fog
from the necessary sea —
Stupid, fatuous men
are not necessarily
all stupid & fatuous,

nor all on the horizon,
nor completely devoid of
good, or hope — The evil
in them will die, the
good will live — Bleak
& friendless universe is
only one of several
illusions, the greatest &
only immortal one of
which is <u>good</u> —
Enough, the words to
this "idea," or belief,
are limited, the combi-
nations to describe it
almost exhausted al-
ready — Manifestations
of this in humanity, there-
fore in your writing work,
are endless however —

This is the return of
the Will

Just the sight of the "snow"
under the locomotive, brings back
sweet light of the boy soul in
Lowell, the human earnest desire
to revisit Lowell this New Year's
& soak up the sad hints of
the past in a grateful soul,
from just . . . "snow" — So
immortal love also hides
in things — talisman details
for the temple soul —
but soul, soul, soul, the
"details" is the life of
this thing —
GO NAKED TO THE WHITE

(End of SK 3)

*   *   *   *   *   *   *   *

EN ROUTE MONTREAL BUS Mar 20 '53

I keep thinking of the
acorn trees outside Lowell
on that gray day Mike
& I hiked to the quarry —
Kirouac will be like
   that, gray, fated —

MONTREAL (in "taverne")
         Montreal is my
      Paradise — &
      they almost didnt
      let me in —
         Railroad restaurant Frisco
         combined with Mexico
         Fellaheen girls taverns
         & Lowell — O
            thanks Lord

                  N.Y.State

            Crows are insane in
            the mist — America
             is thrilling on a gray
             day, Quebec non —
            America has histories
             of wood & Robert

Frost fences—
McGillicuddy'll
make his comeback—
  The Canucks are
    ignorant, vulgar,
    cold hearted—I
    dont like them—
    No one else does—

Moreover <u>Kirouac</u>
  has always been an
unpopular name
among Canucks, for
  Breton reasons I
  guess—something
    hotheaded independent
& brilliant makes
yr paisan bristle
  with suspicion—
      Noel was a whole
      chunk of suspicion
      —I shoulda
        spattered him in
              the street

And that would
tear my clothes
break my watch no
  thanks—

In America the
birch is grievous,
lost, rich, poetic
—the woods are
haunted—a meaning
was united in this
bleak—I know
the dead Dutchman
of Saybrook never
cared for the
name Kirouac—

but I have cared
for ye dutchmen—
It is my prerogative
to believe, in my
own way, in what
haunts my conscience
& fulfills my hope—
I know there's nothing
down the line but
gray indifference, the
earth-covering excrescence
of mean men—
That I was born into

a beastly world with
all the traits in

myself — & God
  will crown my head
  with grave dung —
  but I have sung
  the pale rainy lakes
in this chokéd craw
  of mine & will
  sing again — &
  mine enemies look
    me in the eye
    if they will, or
      be still

                         The moon's
                         dropping a
                         tired pious
                            drape

A Whitman song
 of New England in
   Winter! — the
      coasts, the white
   sprays of shipping off
N.B., the r.r. brakeman's

                         eyes slitting in the
                           long New London dawn
                         — the covered bridges
                         of Vermont, tunnels

of love of old hay
rides in other harvest
moons — The shiney
snake in the bog,
the mad bongoeer
in the dark shore
of Nancy Point —
the blue windows of
mills, of Boston ware-
houses — Wink of Chinee
neon in Portland Maine

A big piece of myself is stuck
is choking me in my throat

My belief in the Holy Ghost
less and less — it's fading
— It must not fade, but
  return — Return, Holy Ghost

March 30 1953

PLANS FOR NEW WRITING
      "Newspaper accounts"
of what happened, short
ones or long "novel" ones,
with moral theme . . . since

that is the final question,
do we live or die <u>bleak</u>.

—Fullscale explanations
in unpausing sometimes
hallucinated prose, of
these things,—
          (No—continue with
          Duluoz Legend)

* * *

Spring in Long Island

Not a blue sky clean
Spring but a mixed
new-haze day smelling
of faint Spring smokes
—a chill wind
makes washlines sway
—a gray horizon, a
radiant sun behind
clouds—in little
snake mottled trees
balls of Spring bole
hang like decorations,
  wave—

Six million diesels
churring & vibrating
  in the yards, waiting
  for fueling   The
  tenderness pale clouds
  that in the exact
  zenith mix with
  the pale pure
    blue — Among the
    bushes the carpet of
    caterpillar hair —
    The basketball
  players of the
  open cement court
      are wheeling &

whistling — a ball's
suspended in air, a
  Scandinavian sweatered
  youth is stiffnecked
  watching it, others
  in attitudes of
  twistback & turn,
    "Ya-y-y-y" —
  — gesturing, talking —
  watchers have arms
on knees — a ball
  is bounced —

A mother works
eagerly in this
  orgone ozone

day pushing a
  teeny child in the
park swing—She
  wont throw him
    down the airshaft
—she says "It's
chilly here"—
    Figures on the
plain of the park
in various throwings,
  strollings, pushings
  of carriages,
scufflings, the
  graceful walk of

                  a beautiful young girl
                  who doesnt care—
                      How can an old
                      man like me
                      devour what she has,
                      it is a nameless
                      newness insouciance
                      & style as ephemeral
                      as gain, as heartbreak-

ing to see as loss
—as lost to
me as smoke
or the smell of
this day—

nothing there is
left for me, for us,
but loss—yet we
choke & gain after
races & rush &
nothing's to come
of it but tick
tack time—
A little paper on
the cement is
just as glad
as I am, just
as won—

Young girls in Levis
with little asses,
little pliant waists
& ribs wrapt in
gray jacket coats,—
green skirts—
I see them walking
off with the huge

L I R R coal bunker
  as their backdrop
  —But yet I
aim to write books
believing in life   How?

In the heat of my
blood it all comes
  out & good enough
  & like birth—
     It still isnt
Spring, the wind
  in my neck's
  not April's,
     March's—
   insistent, beastly,
  knifing—Ah
cars! Ah airplane!

SKETCH

Behind big engine 3669
in the bright day of
  San Luis Obispo the
  mtns. of hope rise
  up, treed, green, sweet
  —a rippling palm

behind the pot steams —
the young fireman of
Calif. waiting to
make the hill up to
    the bleakmouth pano-
    rama plateau of
    Margarita where
    stars of night are holy —

I love Calif. more &
    more — if everyone loved
    it as I do, dear
        abandoned Jack, they'd
        all be here — This
        rippling land was the
        Pomo's — There's
        a cool sea wind
        this noon — With
        F M Hill I'm going
        now to swing the hill —
            to learn — long after
            Neal, & hopeless — a
            strange estudiante
            writer-brakeman

    Only when that work
    which oertops my
        hopeless men-among

                    bones will save me
                 up & back to en-
                    thusiastic inside
                 me personal need
                    breast—

                        The Pomo word for person is animal—

                    So they spoke to
                    spiders & hawks,
                        & thanked the
                        ground they slept on—

SK   <u>People in L I R R Station</u>

     Gray skies, man glances
     at wrist watch,—
     not people—big
   bleak blackwater windows
   of an upstairs Jamaica
     loft with French blinds
     rolled up matted at top
     & bank building marble
     or smooth concrete blocks
     —does God care?
        do I care?

   *

Say What you Want or
        Drop Dead

   You're the boss . . .

        . . .

              Move silently, serpent
              Thru the crisscrossing swords
                 of afternoon
              The shining grass
                Move broadly, servant

              0...0

Sign in Sunnybrae, Calif.: -

        BAY PEST CONTROL
        Our Business is Simply Killing

                        Man is to be a
                        Young animal not
                        an Old carbon copy

NEW!
Brand New!
<u>Daydream Sketch</u>
        Neal & I are in Mex City—

buying tea off queers — we're
   in a hotel room — they
      are very weird, young

                dirty — The hotel is like
              the Hunter, with 2 rooms,
               2 bathrooms, $10 peso
               a day & we're in MC
               only a week just for
               weed & a few Organo
              girls — Neal's blasting
             & rolling & bringing my
                  attention to the weirdness
                 of the boys "<u>Dig</u> them —
              dig their lives, man — The
              way they <u>live</u> — how they
              hustle on that crazy Organo
            street — look at their
              clothes, their eyes — hee
              hee, now dig him, see
          they're talking now, wondering
           how much they oughta charge

us & the little one with
the curly hair & the
  airforce wings on his
   T shirt who's just like
    a little kid — he's

hot for you, Jack — he
doesnt talk business, lets
   old Mozano handle
   that — " & the
mothlike dense eternal
moment of a thousand
   things — caught — I get
   so hi I see the history
   of nation, Indians, America —
   "But Mozano's not
   interested in the money
     either, he's just anxious
     for La Negra to enjoy
     himself — he watches"
Add Achievements: -
   Met Glenway Wescott
in the Kitchen

DEATH OF GERARD

Oil cups flaring in
the misty night, the sand,
   the ditch in the street
with jagged concretes
   of old making little dusty

ledges for little living
strange dusts that are now
blowing in the night —
the flicker of the
flares, the saw horses,
the sand piled —

somewhere on the mysterious
horizon of the suburban
nite like scenes in Mexico
City or Montreal &
equally Strange — equally
weird — equally & O
most hauntingly like
the little man with the
mustache, a strawhat,
a salesman saying he
is dying, the golden daven-
port of his house at the
top of the street —
the wind from the river
cold & inhospitable,
dim lights in houses, creak
of pines, lost Lowell
in a winter night in

1922 & I am not
yet born but the oil cups

flare & smoke in the
night — little rocks on
the pile have eyes —
everything is alive, the
earth breathes, the
stars quiver & hugen
& drool & recede & dry
up & spark — no moon.
Black. Shuffling figure
of a man in a derby
hat handsapockets
going to the latticed
house, the kellostone
pine, the great soul
of my brother in
sadness hums over the
scene — Hear the
river hushing under a
load of ice — Smell
the Smoke of the dump
— the little man in
the strawhat is going home,
newspaper underarm, he's
left the trolley at
Aiken & Lakeview, bot
a new Rudy Valentino
box of chocolates for his
wife for tomorrow night

Friday, I am
dying he said to
me in Eternity in
Montreal years later

& that afternoon Frank
Jeff & I took the 2
girls, sisters, to the
  bleak roadhouse outside
Mex City & danced
to sad lassitudinal
Latin mambos & slow
tempos & tangos —
the rain came, outside
  it was a pine, a gray
window behind brown
pink Mexican drapes
  of decoration — The
  hand drummers dreaming —
I saw the oil cup
  flares of the construction

job at the middle of
  Gregoire St. in Lowell
in a night before I was
born, the moths flying
  millionfold around, the
  dense happiness of

timeless reality and
angels — the incoming
soaring whirlwind
cloud of thoughts, eyes,
the whole shroud, the
Blakean wind &
the voice in the wind
saying "Ti Jean va
venir au monde, Il
va savoir le mystère,
il va savoir le mystère — "
& at the foot of the
street the house where
the woman had an
altar in a room, whole
statue, candles, flowers,
this dame instead of
a TV had in & for her
sittingroom of settees
& kewpie cushions a
bloody sadness in
plaster, loss & vim
of kicking candle flames
hundreds darting to
the rescue in air
screaming pursuit of
lost atoms —

The mist of the night,
the river beyond, the dull
street lamps, the pit of
the universe not only like
the Mass. St of Mary
Carney in another room
   of the Level Time but
   (as dark, as fragrant)
    like the night of
    the dream of the crowd
    playing leapfrog around
     the racetrack with dice,
     knives & interests
   —in Denver, in
    Shmenver, when silently
    I a goof following

 a cop who later turned
into a woman came
padding in my dusty
  shoe of dreams, amazed
—the last gloom, the
last barn—horses?—
  & in the rickety sad
immortal Now-house
   the swarming vision parting
   over the heads of
   little children on the

bed & I'm singing
a saying— "Where's
   Neal?"—& that
      little salesman sipped
his beer in Montreal,
   put it down, adjusted
packages, said "Ben
j m en va chez nous"
   "T'est t un vra
      soulon—"
   "Ben weyon, parl
pas comme ca—On
   dit pas ca—"
   "Aw—" I was
sorry— "En anglais
   en amerique—c'est
   une joke—on dit—"
And he said: "I'm
   half dead anyway—I'm
   goin to die soon" &
off he goes, 98 lbs.,
dark, blessed, off
      into the spectral

Montreal night of
suburban streetdiggings
with oil cups, flares
   illuminating sandpiles,

as the Angel bends
  over, Gerard bends over,
    leering sadly
        in this night—

        – – –

  A great
unequivocal dog
  Is all a wolf is

        I am Mallarmé's
            grandchild
        _____

        The locomotive comes swimming
        thru the newsy city.   In
        a deep cut, houses on both
        banks, full of living lights,
        talk of families in eventful
          kitchens. This is where I come
        riding my Maine white horse.

  A woman in a
Clipper berth foam-
rubber mattress being
served bkfast. in
bed over the jungles of

        Ecuador —
she's going down to Guaya-
   quil as an adminis-
   trative assistant to
some Aid deal — "to
help develop the economic
   'security' etc. of
Indians — etc." — plane
   falls — her thots,
      running, her whole life —
      crash — she ends up

being treated kindly
in a dirty village by
sweet meek Indians
whom she fears — she
   gets hysterical — her
   husband comes to get
   her & takes her back
   to her bedroom in some
   exclusive section outside
Chicago — she's had
   her taste of "Global
   Democracy" "Anti-
   Communism" & all that
      highblown <u>Time</u> shit —
      A movie idea —
      She appears on TV

& you see her lie about
   her "experience" —

   Add to Sam Horn
the idea of modern
   cowboys with Ford
   Mercuries

—————

   Man, the terrible laugh
of those who think
   themselves special
      — élite — it
      has a gory
         hungry sound
            lonely
                  dirty

   Apr 28 '53
San Luis Obispo

   Blue 2 PM Sky
   Mtns smoky
      Growl of motor of
      bigtruck on 101
      Who cares

   Everything is alive
  the blue glass domes
on tphone pole
  The skittering birds
  Rippling palm leaves
  Waving pine branches
    Valley of hope pale
green with dark bushes

A completely pastless
man smoking a
    cig in a dark
    bedroom — fuck
    literature! —
    write like at 18! —
    cracked insanity of
        T & C years
        esply 1948 —
        enjoy — daydreams

Unbroken word sketches
of the subconscious pictures
of sections of the
memory life of an
   imbecile genius resting

in the madhouse of his
mind — The word
flow must not be disturbed,
or picture forgotten for
words' sakes, nor the
pictures stretched beyond
their bookmovie strength
except parenthetically.

Work from your own side of literature
& room fetish, not "publishing's" —
It's the Holy Memory
It's the <u>dinihowi</u> of
Memory
It's fit for dunes &
desert huts & railroad
hotels
Let them pick the story
out of the house of your
words, floor by floor, room
by room

<u>3</u> <u>a</u> <u>Year</u>, <u>like</u> <u>Shakespeare</u>

THE TOWN AND THE CITY	1946–1948
ON THE ROAD	1951
VISIONS OF CODY	1951–1952
DOCTOR SAX	1952
MAGGIE CASSIDY	1953
?	1953

Work on Railroad
DRUNK: Know I can handle it
           (OVERCONFIDENCE)
HIGH: Fear I cant handle it
           (UNDERCONFIDENCE)
SOBER: Know I can handle it
           with reservations
           (NORMAL CONFIDENCE)

Same with work on mind
  & memory —
  Automatic interest in
  that you write what &
  how you like, on spot
  Present tense —
           LIKE

      The following Sketch

Late afternoon in San
  Luis, the Juillard Cockroft
  redbrick courthouse warehouse
  building stands in the
profound 6 PM clarity
  to the stwigger of all
    the birdies — some of
    the birds trill, some sing

like humans — a faroff
racing motor — the still
"suburban" trees — always
the rippling pine fronds,
the breeze — The green
pale grass mtn. with its
  raw earth cut telephone
  pole & scattered cows —

the green dazzle of
grayfence bushes — shadow
of a porch across the
leaves & whitened buds —
Moving shadows of bush
on white house — The
  old Indian's been
  rubbing his antique
    truck all day to get
    the rust rid — now's
    inside working on
  dashboard — That
    sweet little cottage shack,
Southern style groundlevel porch,
  purple flowers in a rock
    front, little slopey roof,
  broom, doormat, with a
    TV in SJ fine —

PEOPLE

"What do you mean,
   There are no people?
   Isnt Hawk people?
   Isnt Dove people?
   And Rat
   And Flint
     And all the rest?"
           —Jaime d Angulo

COYOTE VIEJO

My father in his dying
1945 year thought Danny
Kaye was funny—we'd
   listen to the radio, go to
     shows—how humble in
     eternity can you get?
—We'd sit in the Ozone Pk
parlor on Fri nites listening
to the Pabst Blue Ribbon
Ads between Danny's
   jokes like O Really?
   No O Reilly!—
       & Hal Chase thot
       Danny was funny too
         & that too is a strange

        humility in eternity
— that these gigantic
hearts shd. have latched

onto such a stale &
narrow clown —
      & all for what?
— for waste of time —
    I even used to
listen to Jas Melton,
  dreaming of SERENADE
  by James M Cain,
    just as today I waste
      time on boxscores, on
    Philley's last hit
      or Greengrass's
    homer — or on
        TV stupidities —
how mediocre everything's
got since 10 years!

INTENSITY

Intensity must be all
Ripeness
Intensity is all
All night eager pale
    face Chinatown talk
    in eternity weary
    mystery
      Health is for clams
        snails & shells
        Intensity & sorrow
          is for Geo Martins
          of Time
      For Zagg Big O'Zaggus

ALLEN G.

O Allen Dear Allen
    Ah Allen Poor Me
Walked the streets of
      Ee ter ni Tee
With me —
O Allen Sad Allen Ah
      Mystery — Ah Me
Ghettos
East Sides
Denver Pigeons

Doldrums of Coasts
   Suicides of Seas
         & Hart Crane Sub
         Sea Deities
And Corals & Shelves
Immemorial
         Hallos

   I have nothing to
      say to ye
Except
Dont trod the wrong
      tightrope
Weird Mind will wrassle
      Thee
To a meet in the
      Hole of Destiny
With an Angel White
      as Heaven
   Gold
   Snow
   Cobalt Pearl
   And Fires of Rose
      Then remember me
         long dead.

WM BUTLER YEATS

Stormy mad
Irish Sea
Sex and bone
Cane pipe peat
Death stone
  Constantinople
  Dostoevsky of Machree
  Patriarch of Mayo
    Pard of Innisfree
    Isle of Imagery
      A.E.
      James J.
      Leopold Bloom
    Curmudgeon Connaught
    Patrick O Gogarty Bemulligan
    Silt throat

              —

LONG DEAD'S LONGEVITY

Long dead's longevity
  Coyote Viejo
  Ugly un handsome old
      puff chin eye crack
Bone fat face McGee
In older rains sat by
    new fires

Plotting unwanted pre
   doomed presupposing
 Odes — long dead
   Riverbottom bum
   Raunchy
     Scrounge
     Brakeman bum
     Wine cans sand sexless
       Silence die tomb
Pyramid cave snake Satan

TOMBSTONE

I was a naive
   overbelieving type

AMERICAN CIVILIZATION

Half wanting to live
   Full having to work

       Sketching is successful
         but not fun — not
         artistically <u>absorbing</u>,

like making jerky
    or building a fire
    or writing a
           Cody Pomeray in
         The Poolhalls
or sketching from the mad mind itself

The metaphysical mayor
      broke down

_____

    That which has not
  long to live, frets —
    That which lives
    forever
   Is full of peace
And there is no man who'll live forever
Here it is California,
little young girls going to
school in the fresh &
  dewy sidewalks of sleepy
    San Luis — birds are
    noising up & down —
    a mist sweetens the
    mountains — the cool
   sea beyond the hills
    has been all night
     & will be all day —

ever eating sand, creaming
rocks, washing worlds—
The rail is sticky, wet,
dewy—clean architectural
    trains & perfect red &
    black signals—

my life so lonely &
    empty without someone
    to love & lay, & without
    a work to surpass
    myself with, that I
    have nothing nothing
    to write about even
    in the first clear joy
    of morning—Today
    May 5 1953 I'm
        going to decide on my
    next book—the
    idleness is killing—
        WILL to decide—

    The pristine leader who
made & lost this house
    has none of my sym-
        pathy.

In the desert there was
a sign that said
    "SNAKE CHEF'S
      DAUGHTER DOVE
        XND
    JOSEPH CHARLES BRETON
HERE RECOMMENCED
      THE WORLD
    FROM THE GREAT FIRE OF
      JULY 1845
        URP RAIN AGAIN"
  though no one had seen
  it except the father
of the later generation
Bretons, John.
"Urp <u>what</u> again?"
"Rain"
"What's that mean."
"Nobody knows Looks
like urp. It might
be something else.
  It looks like Snake
   Chef's Daughter Dove.
   It might be something
   else."
    "When did you see
this sign? Why didnt
you bring it with you?"

        "I saw it in 1895
with Uncle Bull Balloon
I didnt bring it I didnt

even touch it. That was
my father's sign your
grandfather He was
given the name Silver
Fox by the Indians His
son his eldest son his
   first was called Coyote
   & is now somewhere in
the Mexican desert or
   walking along a railroad
   track in California
   & known as Whitey to
the bums & Coyote
   Viejo to the Mexicans
   & has a flowing white
beard. That is your
   uncle Samuel He is
   I believe in the
   Zacatecan Desert &

like a ghost."
   "How old were you in
1895?"
   "How should I know?"

"How old are you now?"
"I ceased I dont
count any more I
ceased & deceased . . .
And that little hotbox
in yr car wasnt
even formed in yr
unborn brain cells
when I made my first
payment on this
farce — & you, but
just an idea buried in
dirt at the back of
my brain."
"I remember Old
Jim when his eyes
were moist — "

<u>Sun Apr 26</u> SWING THE HILL

Rent	.90
1 Cream, chips, misc. bum	1.00
I cream	.30
Lost from keypocket	.30
	2.50

(The railroad is a steely
        proposition)

Animals dont have pride
   Men shouldnt — healthy
      men have no peacock
         pride
I've been imitating Gerard
  in reverence since he
    died — his death was
    my one real tragedy
    more than Pa — his
      death my death — But
    imitating & adoring him
    I grew exclusive, special,
    prideful, found <u>Turf</u>, later
    "literature" <u>to</u> <u>do</u> in my room

— in fact life insulting me
because it no longer

included Gerard—
    Get rid of <u>pride</u>
 . Get rid of <u>sorrow</u>
    Mix with the People
    Go among the People,
the Fellaheen not the
    American Bourgeois Middle-
    class World of neurosis
    nor the Catholic French
    Canadian European World
     —the People—
Indians, Arabs, the
Fellaheen in country, village,
    of City slums—an
    essential World Dostoevsky
    if you want to Gauguin on—
but mainly, fulfill yr.
needs, <u>live</u>,—sit staring
in the yard all day, if
the other men laugh at
you challenge them
& ask them if "you would
like it if I laugh at
you"—Screw, drink,
    be lazy, roam, do
    nothing . . . gather yr.
        food—Get out of
        America for good, it's

a Culture holding you,
  no <u>Life</u> — The People
  of No Good & Evil —
  of No Culture, no
    Prophets — nothing but
  essential politics & literature
  as Tales of the People —

Gauguin practised a
neurotic civilization
  impressionism among
primitive fellaheen
  people — is his
  art so good as they
  say? — is it better
  <u>really</u> than all-out
  culture bourgeois dutch
 come-&-honey Rembrandt?
— of course not — Impressionism
is & has always been
  a breakup & compromise
 in the art of picturing
nature & is now a
wild scatalogical paint
blur call'd Surrealism etc

Primitive art nevertheless
is closer to Surrealism

than "Naturalism"
(which is unnaturally tech-
nical) — but primitive
art does not consider
Subconsciousness or
Primitivism — & is in
any case Decoration
for Utilitarian Purposes,
not so called "expression
for expression's sake"
& the difference is
millionfold down deep —
Gauguin would have done
better decorating their pots
& boats — This humility
is the true artist's —

& explains the vast
greatness of Bach writing
for the Sunday Service,
Raphael painting for
the church wall, —
the essential uselessness
of Goethe — Shakespeare
writing to fill the
theater seats — (a
shoddy purpose) —
Homer singing to his

listeners is the essential
fellaheen poet —
    There are 3 basic
possibilities in fellaheen
        Hunter, Priest, Warrior
    The hunter has to be experienced,
the priest political, the warrior
mindless — I'll have to
    learn to be a hunter

The railroad is the hunt
in America, for me (&
    Neal & Hinkle) — hunt
    down the rail for bread —
    I gotta learn many
    essential things now
        —
    Hit my natural male
    level after awhile —
    It aint easy to get
away from the inworked
influence of Civilization
— which is an avoidance
of <u>reality</u> finding its
    greatest symbol in
        embalming fluid —
        Sad that even the fella-
heen are stupid — want

radios & soap operas—
　　Thoreau made the 19th
century intellectual mis-
take of reading the
Koran & the Bible ins-
tead of following his
soul to ultimate . . . the
tales of creation among
the Indians & even
　　further the methods
of hunting & nomadry
—instead he pored over
the stale Goy Hatreds
of the Old Testament,
　　the aristocratic "middle-
class" Arabic cultisms
of Mohammed—
　　The People Need no
Religion, no Art, no War

A healthy man imi-
tating an invalid—
me imitating Gerard—
　　men imitating Christ
　　Cockless Christ—

Culture, & Civilization
its later millionfold

subdivision into
technicalities red tape
   & by laws, is an
incredibly useless clutter
   of substitutes for
sex & real life —
   Anyone interested in
   the million details &
sensations of a Culture
is interested in clutter &

is now (sic) longer in contact
with the Life Flow under-
   neath this junk & there-
      fore Neurotic &
         Dead in Life —
            Reich's Orgone Box
doesnt compare to a screw
   in the noonday sun — nor
      Bogomolets' serum
to sexual & therefore
spiritual (joie de vivre)
longevity —
      Needs from the
earth bleeding — pulque,
cocaine, marijuana,
peotl, gangee, herbs,

woods, vegetables, acorns,
   greens, & the rabbit

  Remember that everything
is alive — the Spider,
   the Rattlesnake, the Tree
     Wish no harm &
none will come yr way
     & tell it to the
        world alive,
          the Animal, the People

     I shall become a
        goatherd — goat
        milk, goat butter, &
        tortillas & beans
           with goat cheese

And yet most of these observa-
tions arise from the fact I
cant get a woman anyhow —
too "bashful," too "scowling" —

     Tho it would be hard
     to surpass the profound
     nostalgia of the smoke
     of an American cigar,
     you would have to sur-

pass it. — To find the
Fellaheen Reality
means to find a
primitive country life
with no morals —
        Country life with
    morals, as in North
        Carolina, is the most
        destructive life on
        earth — City life with
        morals offers a few
    diversions more, nothing more.

Yet whenever I get the
most rigid & philosophising
& dualizing as now,
is when I most weakly
 feel like reacting to
  the allurements of
  what I seek to cast
  out —

  I dont know when
this eternal dual
  circle will end —
    In 1949 it was
  Homestead vs. Decadence
        1951

Mexico City vs. Work in U.S.
1953
Fellaheen vs. America
Be decadent, work in U S &
Have a Fellaheen Homestead too

All is I want
    Love when I want it
    Rest when I want it
    Food when I want it
    Drink when I want it
  Drugs when I want it
The rest is bullshit
    I am now going out
    to meditate in the
    grass of San Luis Creek
    & talk to hoboes &
    get some sun & worry
    where my soul is going
    & what to do & why
            as ever
            & ever
            shit

So that writing will finally
  in me end up to be the
  working out of the burden
  of my education

for personal Surrealistic
self-therapeutic education-
    burden time-fillers in
    Agrarian & Fellaheen Peace

No radio TV education or
papers — a sombrero, a
mujer, goats, weed & guitars

        * * * * * * * * * * *

                    I blame God for
                    making life so
                            boring —

Drink is good for
    love — good for
    music — let it
    be good for
        writing —

This drinking is my
alternative to suicide,
& all that's left

And marijuana
        the holy weed

It isnt anybody's fault
that I am bored—
it's the condition of
time—the burden
of putting up & filling
in with tick tack
time in dull dull day
—How humorous it
is that I am bored,
that it's no one's
fault, that time
is a drag—that I
would rather commit
suicide than go on
being bored—
            Men are new creatures
not built for this old
      earth—the lizard yes

The lizard lost all
his children long before
men began being bored
in this Eden of Harshness

            —

Alcohol, weed, peotl—
      bring em on—&

bring on bodies—
Why does the Indian
    drink?
Because he never knew
how to make himself
  drunk with weeds &
  brews—only stoned

            The carefully exposed
        sipper's bottle is
            suddenly rapidly <u>sinking</u>

Every year be writing 3
    books simultaneously
—a morning sober book
—an afternoon high book
            (the greatest)
—a night drunk book

    hee hee hee!
        & girl
        & friends
    & universal tippling
            forgiveness
WRITE IN SMALL PRINT WHEN YR. DRUNK
The charm of the original drunk—
Vermont—the mtns. of Manchester
& we all got drunk—Kids—tore

up trees — the earth got drunk with
us as I remember — weaving, swaying —

THERE WERE OUTCRIES" " "NASCENCES
OF LOVE***I FELL HEADFIRST
out of the car to greet the
ladies — GJ protected me
& goofed with me in the romantic
American starlit nite of
youth — G.J. — still great
is G.J. — huge-in-eternity GJ —

Goodbye, San Luis Obispo

———————————————————

July 1953

One of those downtown
Manhattan cobble corners
on a gray afternoon
given so much more gloom
to its already gloomy
dimness — the big
busy trucks of commerce
& even occasional horse
teams clattering & booming

by — The corner where
the old 1860 redbrick
now weatherbrick bldg
sags, with Mexican like
sagging black sad broken
sidewalk roof suspended
by bars attached to the
wallfront — it's like

a vision of the old Buenos
Aires waterfront & beater
still & like the bleak
merceds of So America
but the heart of modern
sophisticated Rome-New
York — A rain of
plips & day-mosquitos
falls across the black
dank gloom of the
corner — profoundly hidden
within is an almost
unnamable man on
a crate bent & thought-
ful in the day dark
over his order book &
by mountains of

cabbage crates — The
   gray sky above has a
   hurting luminosity to the
   eye & also rains with
   tiny nameless annoying
   flips & orgones —
      life dusts of Time —
   beyond is the vast
   arcadium green Erie
   pier, a piece of it,
   with you sense the
   scummy river beyond —
   The West Side hiway,
   gray, riveted, steel,
with automobiles crisscrossing
      in the narrow scene
   to destinations like
bright silver ribbons

   North & South in the
   city & no regard, no
   time for the dark sad
   little corner with its white
   oneway arrow, blue St.
   Sign (Washington & Murray)
   leany lamppost, litter
   of gutter, curb as if
   pressed down by years

of trucks backing up —
The lone blue pigeon
trucking along, the
 squad copcar stopping
momentarily to think —
 a scene wherein in
 some darkfog midnight
 2 seamen stagger, or
an anonymous clerk

 in rumpled July summer-
shirt hurries meek
 with Daily News —
 or by gray hot noon
 of dogday August some
 small merchant in
 brown coat, whitehaired,
 clutching a box underarm
 slowly walks — on
  late October afternoon
a rusted & forgotten spot
 in the great joysplash
 of Manhattan with
 its glittering band
 of rivers, ships exuding
  booms, shrouds —
  smoke, of railroads,
 trucks, boom of time

Closer up you see the
actual pockmarked grime
of this sad Manhattan
scene, an old hydrant
with 2 black iron stan-
chions beside it as if
  obsolete ruins of old
  water or horsetrough
  equipments of 1870
when where you now see
  Erie Pier's green parthenonish
  front was the jibbooms
  of great sailing vessels,
    the boom of wagon wheels
    & barrels—Overwritten
doublepainted all-lost
writing friezing around
    the crumbling warehouse

    says BABE HYMAN & SONS
& also DAVE KLYDAN SPE
        interwritten
On the 4th floor, corner
  window, a black hall
  where a pane of less
  blackdusty glass is missing—
  the 5th floor itself is

            home of a savage
poet who lies on his
   back all day staring
   at cobwebs above,
      fingering his beard only
      to — poems on the
      floor covered with dust,
      black dust — his shoes
      a half inch deep in
      dust — not dead —
         yes dead — a Bartleby
      so beat that it

is inconceivable to see
how he can live much
more than 5 minutes —
         The bldg. is for rent —
         The sun comes out,
illuminating the cobbles
   but the grim edifice stays
      gray & wears the
      aspect of the city's
         grave — There
is no poet up there, just
         rats

      & a few sacks

of nibbled-into onion
_ _ _ _ _
urg

LONG ISLAND WAREHOUSE

In the night it's the
great sad orangeness
  of lights shining on
  orange backgrounds for
red letters, like a
  sideshow poster
  the colors but nothing

so flimsy or entertaining—
White creamy huge stucco
warehouse of Kew Gardens
movers, the back of the
  bldg. has silent stairs
  with no one on them
  never at night if ever
  at all, iron stairs that
  lead to a green door
  in the whiteness of the
  stucco wall just by the
  orange & red writing, huge
  half seen half lit

            picture of a truck,
            <u>Chelsea</u>, <u>moving</u>
                phone numbers—
            territorial towers of
            a inexistent Kingdom

that once lived but
 had to be embalmed
 to survive the ages
 & but now in our
 age finds itself
 misplaced as a
 moving company &
    no one notices
    the Algerian splendor
    of those walls
    ramparts creamyness
    & disk Mayan
    designs scrollpainted
    by union brush saw
        hacks on board
            platforms hung up
            & rolled by ropes

2.15 an hour but
not knowing the
Egyptian Kingdom
 splendor of their

work now in the
misty Rich Hill
  night, the
Proustian Goof of
    that thing

Evening, aftersupper
evening in Richmond Hill —
the cool sweet sky is full
of fine little white puffs
  separated angelically
    in regular
— over the tree the
pink hint sensation white
is calm, the tree quivers
  at the leaf — sweet
is the coolness, even the
filmy wire on my TV antenna,
the new transparent aerial
curve is cool, white, blue —
but in the sound & the
sensation the crickets
  muscle whistle, others
  repeat the idiot creek
creek from denser yards,
    cats lap & lick,
    bugs hover, night breathes

sweet soft vastness
into heaven —

the motionless green
grass is like iron, chloro-
phyll, Chinese, densely
personalized, rugged, almost
  pockmarked, rich, as
  if chewed — hanging
  pajamas & rugs on
   lines move majestic
   & slow in a cross
   movement, now they
    hustle a little up —
    flowers blaze in their
    own radium world —
    in night they aureate
    to no human eyes
    unseen magical darts
    of prismatic Violet
    light, for mosquitos

to whir in front of —
Huge purple transparent
  phosphorescent night
  fall now pinks the
  white page of life,
  faces lost in hate

& personal pitbottom
dislikes, hasseled heavy
footed too-much-with
himself man fawdling
in yards of pride,
whining at the dogs
of time, overhead
groans the airplane
of his far reached
folly —

and so the crickets
creek, cree, cree —
eaves darken & get
inky gainst whitened
dusk — the pale
dawn dusk clouds
move not but silent
in a mass advance
somewhere slowly —
it was in evenings like
this I'd lie in my skin
& jeans in California
waiting for the Apoca-
lypse & for Armageddon,
ready, head on lamp,
feet in big shoes,

        pants tight, wallet
      hanky knife tight,

no money no home
  no need but a can
  of beans & the
  responsibility of engines
  on the sticky steel
  rail — As now the
  grape of that
California Wine spread
in the West, shooting
  phosphor glory over
  the Come of the
  World — The
  green weeds like
  with glaze on them
  tough skin as now did
  communicate with
  me a vegetative
    friendliness

Mardou's — the gray light
of Paradise Alley falls
down the draining gray stained
wall with old gray paint

churred windows, outside's
the scream of a little
  girl — The hum big buzz
  city flowing in by thousand
  moth waves — The
    silence of Mardou's
    clothes, the water bottle,
    rumpled bed — face
    American goofing in
    sheets — little sweet
    sad radio — Love
    shoulders of Mardou
Little tree & bush buds on
  the screen outside — some
  are dead little dry ravelled
  quiverers in a dry void —
  some almost that way
    but still organically
    vine likely tangled by strings
    of green life to the twig
    bough of the bush & will
    receive their comedownance
    come October soon —
  some still green & juicy
    lifed, twirled lifelikely
    around on a yellow
    Lonestem to droop in
    the August sorrow of

peace & gas fumes from
hiway—some twig

ends are so small almost
unseeable & bear nothing
but dead leaves who not
only sucked it dry but
had taken a chance &
pitched a mansion of
life there but father-
twig missed, castrated,
cancered out & done
did <u>die</u> so now it's a
pale Indian sticklet
with rorfled dood
leaves bup to dooded
no-life & shake to
quiver of earth on a
general bush bearing
no relation to world
—insignificant, skinny
as sticks in graves—

the big healthy deep
green leaves have et
up all the juice of the
bush, they spring from
elastic stems straight

from the gnarly root-
howa'd bough bone of
the bush-proper &
shake to the wind with
heavy weight & thru
then see the pale
day light in veins
   absorbed to suck
 blushing phosphor greens
   like chlorophyll
—the one recently
stillgreen deadleave
dangling on a broken stem—

East River

   The old blackgarbed
watcher of cities sitting
on the Live Oak Jim
   New York barge in the
   dry cool afternoon—
 watching tugs warp in
   finished excursion boats, river
   tankers, barges pass—
his interest in the river,
   the names of Tug Captains
   & Excursion Steamer deck-

hands, the arrival &
departure of great
ocean going orange masted
like the Waterman
Liberty today docked
at Jack Frost Sugars

across the river in L I City
— This old guy, with
whitefringe hair around
baldspot but wearing his
black soothat, sits on
the bit on the swaying barge,
smoking, — to him the
city & the world is such
a different thing as it is
just across the Drive in
Bellevue Hospital where
in density of world interest
now gloomy psychiatrists
consult with patients &
aint interested in the sun
on the river, the free
gulls floating in the
sleepy tide, the
gay littleboats,

but in problems of
marriage & emotional ad-
justment & all such dark,
gloomy, indoor preoccupations
& with such contempt for
those like those on the
river who dont interiorate
with them in this Byzantine
Vault of Mind Horror—
the walls of Bellevue,
dirty rosebrick grim beneath
shining purities of clearday
heaven, the ink of
the windows, the soot
darkness of the bars in
the windows, the formi-
dable mass & camp
& hangup of the

great structure—& only
beyond, above the white
clean modernisms of a
new bldg. N.Y.U. Medical
Science bldg. there rises
the screwpoint phallus
Empire State Building with
his new TV French

tickler on the end,
 clouds of lost hope,
 sweet, impossible, pass
  behind it high, there
 the interests of millionaire
 corporations high above
 the tangled human streets
 —old Live Oak Jim
aint interested in but just
the river & that

 Lehigh Valley barge
with the 2 cuts of cars
being loaded, meeting of
railroad & seawater rail
 to railpoint in the
 actual workingman
 afternoon of the real
 world—And yet
  above all, the mystery,
  Live Oak Jim really is
  an old ex Bellevue
  mental patient, flipped
   in '33, knows it well,
   has his back to it now
   in studies of his river,
   —now's inside napping,

his brother is a lawyer
in the Empire State Bldg.

Black Tanker

   Gloomy black tanker
being tugged in, the gray
  superstructure as tho they
 hadnt in 10 years yet
 scraped the war paint
 camouflage off, the
 blue stack with white
 "T" — the black
sinister hull, — "Michael
 Tracy" — deck gang
   chipping hatch covers
  upstood — stewards
  huddled at stern in
   idiot white, watching
    waters — "I'm
  gonna git drunk
            tonight!" In from
                Persian Gulf

New York Panorama

The UN Building with
white marble side, little
    laddrs of workers strung
up the side — Queensboro
Bridge with archaic
pinpoint boings & big
  superstructure with
  minute traffic & looking
  Chinese in the
    sod besoiled soot
  stained cleanpale
    lateafternoon sky —
  the river tide swells
  & is somber below
    the sad slow parade
  of truckforms & car
  insects inching to the

Eternity — In Long
  Island City antique brewery
red oldbuildings like
    Jamestown in 1752,
  steeples, wine red ware-
  house pier, orange clean
stacks of ships —
  1837 written on a huge

grim dirtybrick gallow-
   house nameless iron
   rack cluttered warehouse
   lost unknown blood
brick factories spewing
smoke — behind them
   other smokes of further
   dim cement rack
   factories pale & vague
   as dawn in the pale
   worm of the sky —

   rosy clouds above — like
   off the coast of Manzanillo —

Subway Sensations

   Smell of burnt nuts
in the power of the
car & the aromatic
almond dusts of the
   tunnel — Growling
   whine of the shurry
   moveahead car as
      it balls from one
      station faster light-
      flashing to another

till wasting the
brakes crash to
stop & the whine
amid knocks &

wheel bumps lowers, till
the stop, the doors,
the bump, the
restless churry churry
wurd wurd wurd of
the power as it waits
to resume — cars
swaying, vestibule sway-
ing — The switch
point ta tap too boom
like a song crossing
another track on
bumpy parts of
track — The Mexico
cafeteria tile of
station walls — the
start-up again, the

growing whur of the
power to fly another
black halfmile with
smashing crossings of
posts & dark reel-

by of pipes, lights,
concrete curbs, darkness,
Egyptian mummy niches,
    till the station
again,
        the "Quick
Relief Tums And
Indigestion" sign

MY MOTHER'S FRENCH CANADIAN SONGS

TI SAUVAGE NOIR

C'est un ti savage noir-e
Noir tous barbouillez wish-té
S'en vas' t' a la rivière
C'éta pour se baigner wish-té
Tou-ma-né-got-a-wilta
                wilta
Tou-ma-né-gét-a-wilté
                wilté
Manégé — wish-té

De la premiere-e plonge
Le savage a chanter wish-té
De la second-eplonge
Le savage c'ai baigner wish-té
Tou-ma-né-got-a-wilta

<pre>
                        wilta
        Tou-ma-né-gét-a-wilté
                        wilté

        De la second-e plonge —
        Le savage s'ai baigner wish-té
        De la troixieme plonge
        Le savage c'est noyer wish-té
        Tou-ma-né-got-a-wilta
                        wilta
        Tou-ma-né-gét-a-wilté
                        wilté
</pre>

ÉLANCETTE (sung fast) (Caughnawaga Indian)

<pre>
        Élancette me tonté   (Song)
          Ma ka hi
         Ma ka haw
         Baisser
        Ma ka hi cawsette
        O bé go zo
        Ma gou sette-a
</pre>

BUTTER SONG

Encore un ti coup
Ça raidit toujours
Vire la manivelle

Mamoiselle
Mam-selle-a
Encore un ti coup
Ça raidit toujours
Vire la manivelle
Mamoiselle
Ç'est tous

* * * * * * * * * *

New York tenement
window sill, they want to
hold nature close to their
lives, they have pathetic
little pots with dead
roots & stems — One
tiny earthen pot sits
in an asparagus can,
its produce is 2 stems
with dry dead leaves
fawdling houseward &
as tho falling in —
Another clay pot
has a completely just
died green that has
shot up & then

down to die on the outside
at the base of the pot
the stem completely bent
& despairing—Two name-
    less blackpainted tin cans,
    small ones, former frozen
    orange juice cans, with
    just dry white earth in
    em—A larger black
      can with nothing in it—
      A tiny new-shining clay
    pot with a little
        fwit hollow stalk
          like dead cornstalk
          sticking out—Another
          clay pot with a
sprig of last Autumn's
 dead leaves torn with
 a stem from some
tree it would seem—
One final jar with a
   kind of scallion looking
   green growth the only
   live thing in the sad
   window the sill of
   which is incredibly
   chipped dry slivery
   wood painted onetime

      sick blue — the
   window frame sick
      green — The inside
   wall bilious yellowish
   with stains — the
      outside wall of the

building at that point
   out in the back alley
a kind of stucco cement
with gaps showing
underneath concretes
— the sill's outer
extremity is a slab of
   rock — Here in the
      hot dogday last days
      of August the windowsill
         hangs in bleary reality
      meaningless with cans
      & dry roots beneath
      an open unwashed wind-
      owpane, clutters of
      wrinkled huskleaf that
      suddenly jiggle in a
         breeze —

The person who has it
is off to work, his

handiwork window in
  the great symphony of
NY throws one mite
  little note into the
  general disharmonious
    irrationality of the
  world & its world city,
as pathetic as a
    job, useless as tight-
  lipped mute unhappiness
  of people rising on rainy
  Sunday afternoons to
    their further tasks of
    carrying the burden of

time to a conclusion they
cannot know & would
not want to know
  if they knew — the
  junk in the window
  is like a young woman's
  disappointed eyes on
  a rainy Sunday, in the
draining dank gray room
  of tenement life, her
  sad feet shiftless, the
  hang of her thoughts,
    the angel of gray

brooding reality, the
Guardian Angel over
    her sorrow, over

her little humilities
as humble as clay pots,
modest as dead
    stalks & fallen vines,
    —as strange & somehow
pathetically sweet as
those little frozen O J
    cans painted black
        by concerned hands
    in a moment of
        serious press-lip'd goof
    in this Open Void
        World forever so
    nostalgic with the voices
        of men
        singing

for nothing & all lies—
idealistic lies of love—

"Men are tricky-tricksy"
        —D. H. Lawrence, a
    facetious Englishman who

stumbled on a serious truth
about love.
  "Yr. mainspring is broken,
Walt Whitman." —
  Whitman should have lived
so long to hear an
  irrelevant English tubercular
  snarl thus at him as at
  a cocktail party in
    Manchester

"The Mystery of the Open Road"
          or
    "The Road Opens"

  Great quote from D H
    Lawrence whom I just
    castigated & underestimated

"Stay in the flesh. Stay in the
limbs and lips and in the belly.
Stay in the breast and womb.
Stay there, O Soul, where you
belong—" <u>D. H. Lawrence</u>
    in "Studies in Classic
    American Literature"
    . . . on Whitman . . .

The thing that eludes —
the working walls of
  America, the dry yards,
  the nameless meeoos
  and micks you hear in
  the night as if cats
  were being bitten —
The endless decision of
streets.
  like when he waded thru
  that New Mexico flood &
  lay down soaking in a
  raw old gondola, trying
  to light fires, & the
  water all around the
    boxcars of the
      drag

        Bring Visions of Cody
            to Cowley

Sunday Night TV

Ed Sullivan looking at
audience with big dumb
nod as they applause
  young girl singer with
  sexy female laff—
    audience applauds as
    Ed inveigles them
    further, says "Tre-
    mendous job"—long-
    faced serious facing
    Sunday night millions
    as my mother in

kitchen bends tongue on
lips tying her garbage
  bags carefully from
  roll of strong brown
  twine, she pauses mo-
  mentarily to see TV
    set from the side with
    an expression of
    skeptical peering curio-
  sity—"T's a
      Nigger?" when a
      baritone comes on, with
      huge voice, she

comes up winding string,
says, "S got a
   good voice huh?"
   as outside in America
   cars gleam dully in

the August heatwave
Sunday night of
humidity no breeze,
  the trees hanging leaves
  still as stone, airplanes
passing in the overhead
Long Island softness &
  the Negro is singing
  "Because," little mustache
  touching almost his nose
  as he says — "to
  me" — clasping hands
    to finish, little hanky
    in suitcoat —

MY CAT

  Kittigindoo sits
on his haunches on the
cement drive in the
  shade turned half
  around listening—he
  now with pricking
  ears is looking up at
    house windows, eyes
    green & dissatisfied
—when I call him
      he is in a
    trance looking strait
    ahead & his ears
      prick & he moves
      his little mouth—

Sometimes he hangs
his head & sulks with
muscle neck, then
yawns, then moves
slowly tail a-
poppin—He loves
  to eat & lick his
  chops & paws—He
  moves with the majesty
    of a gigantic tiger

only to sit again,
  lick at his paw &
  look up — I wonder
  how he makes the
  afternoon, the day,
  the time of life

& its whole long
burden there with his
  tail & paw lickings
  & chest nibblings &
  cheek-diggings-with-
  foot & neck-workings
  with lowered tense
  body right paw
  supporting him — how
  he overcomes boredom
  & the burden of time
  even in his 8 year
  lifespan (which is
  so long).
His isolateness in
  the world, the
ripple afternoons —
  little shadows of
windows at his

soft white feet,
  the dumb pricking
    rueful realizations
    he has crossing the
  green span of his
  eyes & the lowered
  pause & male wonder
  of the Fall, the
  consternation of
    lookup, the chew
on claws with gritting
greek teeth, the
long contemplative
lick on long upheld
  back leg—

The green eyed
slit & stretch of
forepaws & back
up, y-a-w-w—
Mangy, he keeps workin
  on that ear of death
—I noticed in
  him seeds of mange
  last winter on my
  poetry desk (MAGGIE
  CASSIDY)—Now he
  regardant reclines

to continue the day
in the breeze &
sweetness, clear
    time opes around

him, unperturbed he
flicks his sore ear &
mulls, rumes, moons,
mokes, mulges with
himself the long
dread afternoon that
old humans kill with
beer or cubab —
the honest innocent
clean all suffering
cat, no kicks or
drugs available his
supple sad body,
    just lies there
    waiting for the
    end of his 9 years

or 5 years — waiting
without comment,
complaint or com-
panion — licking
    his fur in the bleak,

with no expression —
   listening, pricking,
watching, waiting,
 cleaning himself for
 the Day of the Lord
    O Smart Not
       Crazy!

Saturday Afternoon Window

RO-LET —
   Raw   Bay   Whom
   Debt   Gush   Big
   Hums   Worm   Year
   Yogi   Tide   Dust

(Imp.)   Him   Gum
Hay   Duty   Bids
Mows   Robe   What
Diet   Wags   Yore
Grub

   Tomb   But
   Hug   Wigs
   Wire   Home
   Days   Yard

Bugle bubble blower—
freckled kid bubbling—
Sad lill blue yellow
rubber wallct—
Bldg. blocks half inch
thick—"Junior Arch-
itects" bldgs blocks—
  Star Stamper,
    lill girl stamping *'s
Lil pickaninny penny
  dolls with safety pin,
    cloth, lil red cherry lips
in black face—Lil
plastic bulldozers—
  Tiny Tim bicycles—
  Nickles Dimes Quarters
  Amt. Dep. cash register
    plastic black—
Nameless old halloween
  fluff papers—baby
  carriages big as yr thumb—
    Lil boy in jeans &
    stripe jersey whistles
    Pop Goes Weasel

at this window—Plastic
tiny oldtime locomotive,—
—Bronx prrt'ers

saying Japan—
Plastic bags of
dull samesize marbles—
Sad goggles with garter
holders & canvas—
Play money $25,000 bills
—ray guns—rubber
        guns—big

pearl handle champ
  guns—rubber cigars—
rings with monkey
  on face—Italian
    tenor singin somewhere—
Rubber Knives—(black
  handle silver blade)
    Solar Commando Gun
with Darts—
  Handcuffs of little
      tin & boy
        policemen with

captain badge &
    whistle—Sad
    plastic flesh pale
    lil doll falling back
    naked in a brown
    paper box with

a tiny mouth
    harmonica "Robin"
—Fishing hooks,
"You land the big
ones every time with
    Ole's Genuine

Fishing hooks fashioned
by experts of
Finest tempered
  steel, specially imp-
  orted" —Plastic
  lil Space Ship, &
  imitation lead Space
  men —Jump ropes
  with red wood
    grips—

Expensive Nin toy
    dish set—cups
    & saucers, spoons,
with sad lil yellow
  designs braided on—
  Tiny pushdown
  tops priced in
  black 19¢
  & shows lil boy
  kneeling in toy

colors in lost
        void—

Volga Inn   Music
  Ez tu p a va
   tez - tomata
   - tomata—
Ami topy oll
     mayay—
     Ena oo ee
     Peñooti ma
       ya govin
     Oora pey

(Meanwhile night in
its October form soft
as Indian silk
  slink in the door
    dark, glitters of
    New York night be
    saddening & showing
    where leaves do
      jiggle & bloss bluff
on boughs' come Autumn
"dominant" doom
   —King Size
    first in Sales!
     First in Quality!

First in Good Taste,
—there's yr iron
bars of the park
shine shadowing on
the cobbles of
the oldworld tired
street—There's
the halo lamp
making seen the
goldhair backnapes
of Jacky O Hara's
bestlastfirst
doll—Minnie
Gallagher—

& that sensation
in the pricking gut,
of winter, rivers,
ships, aye ye
green city &
grand land onrolling
it—
Hail Hail the
Gang's all Here,
in Polka, bruits
in the juke—
oonyateez tey
ayetez with

muddy boots' been
    done

3rd Ave Bar

  4 PM the men
are all roaring like
  the EL in clink
    bonk glass brassfoot
    barrail 'where ya
goin' excitement—
    October's in the
    air, is the Indian
    Summer sun of door
—2 executive
salesmen who been
  workin all day
    long come in

young, welldressed,
    justsuits, puffing
    cigars, glad to
    have the day done
    & the drink comin
    in, side by side
    march in smiling
    but there's no

room at the roaring
(Shit!) crowded
bar so they stand
2 deep from it
waiting & smiling
& talking—

Men do love bars &
good bars shd. be
loved—It's full
of businessmen,
workmen, Finn
MacCools of Time
—beoveralled
oldgray topers dirty
& beerswiggin glad
—nameless truck
busdrivers with
flashlites slung
from hips—old
beatfaced beerswallowers
sadly upraising

purple lips to happy
drinking ceilings—
Bartenders are fast,
courteous, interested in
their work as well

as clientele — Dublin
at 4 30 PM when
the work is done,
but this is great
NY, great 3rd
    Avenue, free lunch,
smells of Moody
    St exhaust river
lunch in road
of frime by-
    smashing

the door, guitarplaying
 long sideburned heroes
 smell out there
 on wood doorsteps
 of afternoon drowse
—but it's N.Y.,
 towers rise beyond,
 voices crash
mangle to talk
 & chew the
gossip till Earwicker
 drops his load —
    Ah Jack Fitz-
    gerald Mighty
    Murphy where are

you? — semi bald
    blue shirt tattered
    shovellers in broken
        end dungarees
    fisting glasses of
    glisterglass foam
    top brownafternoon
    beer — The El
    smashes by as
    man in homburg
    in vest but coatless
        executive changes
        from right to
    left foot on ye
    brass rail —

Colored man in
    hat, dignified, young,
    paper underarm,
    says goodbye leaning
over men at bar
    warm & paternal
    — elevator operator
    around the corner —
    & wasnt this
    where they say
    Novak the real
    estater who used

to stay up late
  a-nights linefaced
  to become right

        & rich
in his little white
worm cellule of
the night typing
up reports & letting
wife & kids go mad
  at home at ll
    PM—ambitious,
    worried, in a little
    office of the Island
    right on the street
    undignified but open
      to all business &
      in infancy any
      business can be
        small as

ambition's big—
pushing how many
  daisies now? &
never made his million,
never had a drink
with So Long GeeGee
  & I Love You Too

in this Late afternoon
beer room of
        men excited
        shifting stools &
        footbottom rail
        scuffle heel
            soles —

Never called Old
Glasses over & offered
  his rim red nose
  a drink — never
  laught & let the
  fly his nose use
  as a landing mark
—but ulcerated
  in the middle of
  the night to be
  rich & get his
  family the best
—so the best
  American sod's
  his blanket now,
  made in upper
  mills of Hudson
    Bay Moonface
        Sassenach &
carted down by

housepainters in
white coveralls
(silent) to rim
  the roam of his
  once formed
flesh, & let
worms ram—

    Rim!
  So have another
  beer, topers—
  Bloody mugglers! Lovers!

Crazy Old
  Homehouse of
        the Sea
    & Drowse Afternoon

    At 28th St
& East River
  —the great
    seagoable hull

of iron is mossed,
in green at the forever

waterline — The anchor's
unrusted, gray, white
 bars, balls — unused
— Ah the
wood sides & hall
 windows & Navy
 contests inside —
  the dormitory row
  of it! — the
  madhouse barnacled
   paint fleckchip't
   gull shadowed
  bulk huge of it!
the pissing shovel
 scupper — voices
 in the helm, ghosts
of Billy Budd, old
 EastSide dreams,
  the blue Navy
   flag — the
   side doors & open
   D a w i o v t s
        Handel French
    joywindows of
      winter it!
     — preliminary
    worrying draft &
     study of it!

Something sad, Whitmanian
& Navy-like —
gulls — that same
afternoon hotdrowse
of gulls & slapwater
dream I noticed
in 1951 getting sea
papers & 1942
too — the Melvillean
youth dreaming in
sea pants, at
his clerical dockside
work — with night
to come — the
Turkish bath madnight
& cunts
in parks — The
house where all
the sad eyed
Okie sailorboys
in T Shirts
madly sleep
— The long
dream eternity and
afternoon madhouse
solemnity of it!
— the long planks
& Colonial windows

on the actual water
  of the living
(When the H bomb
  finally hit NY
one afternoon the
  first living act I
  saw was a man
  surreptitiously pissing
  while lying on his
    side)

Dream Sketch

Some doctor is talking
to us about the guy
who broke his leg
clean in half—
we've just seen
  him hobbling around
with a curious limp,
  some old guy not
Neal— "He'll
walk alright in a
  few months but
  come 55 & 60 &
  it'll reappear &

be pronounced —
   the <u>nerve</u> is

affected when you
snap yr leg clean
   in half like that!"
—I think of
   Neal & the hobble
   he'll have at 55
—

<u>Paradise Alley</u>

   October in the
wash hung court —
   wash pieces flip & kick
in the cool breeze,
   on the radio's the
   excited World Series
   voice & the name
   Ally Reynolds
   (secretly smiling Indian
   padding back to
   dugout) —
airplane drone above
in the buzzing world
   afternoon of Lower

East Side — someone
whistling — hone buzz
hum of Vibratos Man-
hattoes in Million
blowers humming in
   the Void Wait Time
— kids battering, yelling
— a little red wagon
   hung from a hook —
   a moan, nameless
   <u>speetz</u>, the rack of
      French blinds being

pulled — October in the
   Poolhall, the clack of
   a sodapop box no
   balls click <u>till</u> big
      dense swarmnight —
   all this so well &
   good — Somewhere a
      motor straining —
      nylons waving — a
   crazy inside-deep
   high thin Porto Rican
   monkey rapid
      woman chat blatter-
         ing "Yera mera quien
         te tse que seta . . ."

Too independent to go
be begging at
anybody's ports
for more than a
        month

———

Plucking at
Her ha! — harpstring

—

To whom rapture
        means
    rupture

Oct 13 1953

Applied for job at
Jersey Central — offered
ground switchman
job, stand in cold
winter lining
switches & sending
kicked or humped
cars rolling down
various tracks — bleak
— healthy —
$100 every half —
4, 5 days a

week — Plenty kicks
with Mardou, plenty
   jazz, wood for

fireplace & dig the
big NY this winter —
Spectral Ole
Jersey Central is
like the SP
at 3rd & Townsend,
right on water where
rail meets river —
sea actually —
now I have coffee
in JCRR lunchroom
& remember 1951
   Xmas the Harding
   at Am Pres Lines
   Pier — etc. —

A barge graveyard
   outside J Central
   yards — NY Skyline
   of Wall St high &
   serene in pristine
   October afternoon —
   October sits
      golden on the

iron old wood &
white gulled
rivers — The
Statue of Liberty her
weatherbeaten green
beak close looming
over sunk barges,
pier, masts, in
spokeless blue —

ferns ghost swiftly
in the channel —
excursion lowboats —
This old barge teeters
at angle, abandoned
coverless stove, stovepipe
still in, still a lot
of dry dust coal,
table, colorlost
chair — the barge's
bottom is sunken
mosquito hive &
tenement of beams
bird limed &
boards flowing in
tarn, the tenement
of gulls!

unspeakable hidden
home, they all
 flap flocked when
 they heard me
 crank up the board
 plank — Big
    iron black bits
    still solid in barge
 deck — The broken
    barge deckhouse is
    like shacks under
    Denver viaduct last
    summer — instead of
    weeds, tarns of
    green bilge slime
       & one old soaked
          mattress of gray

— chick gug gug
 Keree Keree of
some crane motor
nearby, insistent calls
    of tugs — I saw
    shrouds freighters
    standing in the Bay
 — harbor — The
    S of L, her back,
    her torch upheld

to a smoky uncaring
  strife torn waterfront
    striking Brooklyn —
    Barnacled gulled
piers standing in
  low water as the
  old piles of

ancient Princeton
  Blvd Lost Generation
roadhouses with river
porch dancefloors &
  oldtime lamps with
  tassels & beer of
    yore — October's
    little falling white
puffs from giant
    weedfields —
      Jerseyward the
gloomy men in rubbage,
  the smoke of
  old switch pots,
    industrial & sometree
    horizons in the
        October Gold —

I'll live on the
West Waterfront,

—be Wolfe
   —on a day like
this exactly 12 years
  ago I grabbed
  her golden cunt the
  moment she jumpt
  into the car in
    Manchester Conn.—
       I was 19, horny,
    October Gold was
    on the hill then
       too—Oil
     in a map trance
     slowly passes,
     pockmarkt shit

with it—a
ruined submerged
bedspring like the
dump in Lowell
   a giant 20 foot
plank moves over
  like a long dead
  snake waiting
    for the sea—
   —warm sun,
peaceful distant
   smokes maybe of

hospital boiler rooms
—nameless faroff
yowls of trains—
    Swaying newbarge
      orangepainted
—the great ships
fatbottomed crooked
stern strange at
the foot of Man-
hattan bulk
  walls—the mystery
of their world going
hulls slightly slanted
& tied up at the
  doorsteps of Time
  & the World City
—Good God
the great ocean
one way sparkling
wine white to   dry
  red Spain sunrise
    to come—

& all the green
  harvestland t'other
way, to other San
  Joses—other yards—
    blam!   be-krplam!

the running slack
  sk-c-l-to-clank
 of a cut being
rammed or braked
 & I saw the yard
brakeman riding head
 high in mid air
   over emptyreefer
   lines — The
   rusty playwheels
   of the railroad all
   waiting for me   Ah

The long blood dozes

3 POEMS
OCEANS KISS

Oceans Kiss in
Land that lips
Encompass with suck
Of love Immortal
Under the moon
  Of America sick
  And pale blond
  Ashen tuberculosis
In Sanatoriums of

Colorado
Far in the Wild
Essential Indian

DAWN

Dawn's gray birds
Herald hoppéd Angels
Broken-backed
From fucking all night
With San Remo
Queers Intense
  And Eager to learn
The latest Literary
Avidity — Came
Chirping to Envision
Horror, Teach it to
  The Millionaire in
  The Rail road Hair

OOPS

Poets were Glad
When Success a Smile
  Sent Wine-like
Smile Warming
Their way but when

Dross Failure Rain
& Doom of Exciting
Gray Day Coal Chutes
Enveloped Again
They thought they
Had to Go to Work
Instead — a
Successful American

★

Let us see which of
these leads writes best
in the softly applied lap
touch originated in 1912
by Swim Ward B. Thabo —
President of the Acme
Industrial Foundation
makers of Corsets for
Model T Fords in the
Nebraska Primavery —
For by applying the light
touch in the manner which
you see here prescribed
something of the Primavery
is retained & pre
served like Pen
shades

"Sketch" Sunday Afternoon NY

The great bulk of Wall
  St you'd think'd make
the lower tip of Manhattan-
  toes sink is rising pink as
  salmon on the edge of the
  blue mouth harbor waters
  as you see it from the sad
Jersey Central Ferry — about
4:30 PM, long sorrow rays
  hide between the cold
  uncaring-of-human walls
of Wall St but there's a
  heart beating in the rock
  somewhere — in the
breasts of little girls coming
  on the ferry in little

ribboned hats & lacy
drawers & Go to Communion
  shoes their eyes avid wild
  to see the big world & learn
& to understand how their
  happiness is to be secured
  from the Macrocosmic Stone
  of Awful Real, how at
  least they can adjust to

it just as the dying fish ad-
   justs itself to the swerve
   & swerveback of the waves
 —awright so we're all
gonna die but now is the
   time to sing & see, to be
   humble, sacrificed, late,
   crazy, talkative, fool-
      ish, mailteinnottond,

   crawdedommeeng,
all the cross megoney's
   & followsuits to be
   mardabonelated or Bug,
 —they'll be saying you
   lost yr touch & you're only
a one day old Balzac
   on Sun Oct 18   1953
                     balls

   Time, rather, to be proud,
indispensable, early,
   sane, silent, serious,
not mailteinnottond at all

Death of Gerard

The original late afternoon
   of Fall when I was in
      a wicker basket crib
         & parked on dusty skinny
      wheels at that long gray
      concrete garage with edi-
      ble looking blockstones creme
puffed & as if puddinged
      to cook & eat & unforget-
      table in the One Reality,
      the sun has warmth in
      it (& the single twick
      of a little November
         bird hid in the twiggish
         branch on the other
         side of the cool
            redpink lateday

air) — & I'm swaddled
   to the eartips in pink
   Fellaheen swaddling clothes
with rose cheeks & poor
   morf mouth muxed to
   see the day — a drone
      of 1922 Fall airplanes
in that unrecoverable bleak

& the river's old man
  in the valley bed wailing
  arms out elbowed to
    swell the muff of
    shore aside & on, carry-
ing junk fenders to
    the cundrom's drowned
    immaculate cove
    of oil sticks under
      the Boott mill door

walls where eyes of
  drowned boys mix with
  ink rags & sweat of
  dye vat devils with aged
  mothers at home dependent
    & enduring like yon
    sadchild in basket the
    wait of the late red
      afternoon to see what
Paradise will bring—the
  sun fairly warm, the
  air cooling to supper—
  the pines scenting toward
  winter where black
    sledders will swirl
  the dizzy sticks

in traceried Netherlander
fields & I shall see
  Gerard float down
pinkhappy to yipe in
  the few-year'd
  mystery of his days,
Nin behind him — the
heat of the faint red
sun on the garage wall,
on my basket, & I
  lay in T like awe
eyes fixed on the in-
credible immortality
of fadebrown almost
pink clouds salmoning
  motionless in their
    singed Nov. blue —

simultaneous with voices
from a passing car &
the croo croo ack sudden
yark yipe bark of
  a big pup attendant
  on some turmoil in his
sight & part of plain,
  so I lie there (& far
  off now, antique fire
    crackers of last July

of back fart of pipes
of trucks or torpedoes
on rr track, echoing
far, like skaters near
Lakeview Ave.)—
all Lowell waits,
the Kingdom, all

earth, for the babe's
comprehension—for
someday I shall be
king, & lord over the
hollows & corridors
of my mind in
divine memory's
sincere recall
Prince of my own Peace
& Darkness—cultiva-
tor of old soils for
new reasons—here
comes my mother, the
basket quivers to
roll—the wheels do
sweetly crunch

familiar Autumnal
dry ground of little
leaves & dry sticks

of grass & flattened
containers & cellophane
crumples & coal pebbles
& shinyrocks & dusty
old graydirt scraggles
pebbly gritty like
the living ground I
would get to see 3000
miles & 30 years later
in the railroad earth
of California — home
we roll to supper —
I see a redbrick wall
before returning little

face to final pillows
so by the time I'm
undone out of the basket
& put to bed in the
house I'm asleep &
dont know & the
world goes on without
me, as it will
forever soon —
My sweet Father
with sincere eyes &
out stuck ears is
in a tight dark

suit hurrying beneath
   the filament tracery
   blacktrees in
      pale blue time

to get to the last
client & hurry on
   home — Nin's on
the porch, red cheeked,
playing with splinters —
   Gerard broods in the
   dank parlor in brown
swarm holy late
   day dimness, thinking,
      "Gerard whom
         the angels of paradise
shall save from the
iron cross & make
   friends with God, on
   his side, hero, saved,
   despite all sins of
      dizzy now" —

"Gerard qu on va
amenez aux anges
      avec des lapins,
      des moutons, des loups,
      de tite filles, des

tite souris, des
morceau d'terre,
        Ti Jean, Ti Nin,
        Papa, Mama, les
            anges de la souterre,
les anges cachez dans
cave, les giboux dans
l'cemetierre entour
    du sidewalk, les
        giboux dans la
        lune Indian, toute

ensemble avec
    les crapauds au
    ciel et on
    va toute chantez —
    je sera mou pour
    prier dans la
    creme au pied
    dun throne de Dieu,
    ma tete pendu sur
    un aile chaude
        toujours pi apres
        Mama viendra me
        cherchez joindre
            tous —"

TRANSLATION NEXT PAGE

"Gerard whom we shall
bring to the angels
 with rabbits,
 lambs, wolves,
  little girls,
  little mice,
  pieces of earth,
   Ti Jean, Ti Nin,
    Papa, Mama, the
    subterranean angels,
the angels hidden in
 the cellar, the gibberers in
  the cemetery beneath
   the sidewalk, the
    gibberers in the
     moon, all

together with
 the frogs to
  heaven and we
  shall all sing—
  I'll be soft for
  praying in the
  cream at the foot
 of the throne of God,
  my head leaning on
  a warm wing
   forever and then

Mama'll come
find me joining
all — "

SUNDAY IN THE YARDS

Along the rusty track in
  throbbing pink twilight that
casts a faint veil glow on
the iron blackbound soot &
coal, 2 tank cars & 4 coal
hoppers tied in one unmoving
drag, waiting mute under
  the soft November moon of
New York for voyages that will
  take them to nostalgic plains
  of snow in the great land
  west — those same rust
  bottomed wheels will roll
    & clack over switchpoint
    ticks of other rails, drive
    hard rust mass to new
  Idalias somewhere &
where you'll see the rose
jawed freezing brakeman
standing by a North Dakota
  spur in a blizzard with

his gloved hand momentarily
at rest on the old hopper
handrail, spitting, cursing
"When the hell they coming
back anyways! I got
to put a meal of pork
chops inside my belly before
this local Godforsaken takes
us further away from the
last restaurant — " — he
wants to eat, be warm,
drink coffee — but

stands in great weary
America which I see now
haunted redpink in the
west & a parade of shadowy
boys handsapockets walking
along the boxcar tops
in the vast delicate dusk
traceried by trees of the
living looking like little
jigglets & little Coolie
Chinamen howling for
the Formosa, their feet
topping down the singsong
walkways along which I
used to run puttin pops

up & down — As
if this was what a

man would want to write
who has nothing left to do
in his life but keep his
joy in secret scribbled note-
  books — no, I'll have
to try again, start all over,
  again — Enthusiasm
   is a design that has to
   be re-woven in this
    bare barking heart, I
    hate my life now not
    love it, damn
        Leaves dont respond,
   sticks lie broken,
     dead leaves gather dust,
     the West reddens
       & narrows cold
the moon mawks to
purse her still lips —
  lavender over the lights
of supper home, — wind
sweet memoried of
  California, I die, I die
when I am not enthused
  & full of meek ragged

joy, please dear God again!
    The prayer of my
mother that I need
    a father, answered!

"Enthusiasm is a design
that has to be re-woven
    in this bare branch heart"
    says the Goddam
    motherforsaken fop

who calls himself Kerouac
& cant even slurk up & slack
slop out them old jaw crack
& spit, flurp, I'm gonna be a
writer if I have to be a
    goadamn bom bum mopping
    up the shithouses — of —
        Ah — go on with it, Jean,
        Jack Kerouac, & no more
        foppery, jess plain western
        talk is what I say &
        let me see them boxcars
    in the moon of real N
    Mexico — fags hanking
        back their asses in Sun-
        day afternoon ballets, to
        show they aint just

cocksuckers but know all
   about art & studied—
      (advertise themselves as
coming from Europe, to
impress old Queens of Ozone
   Park Ladies, & have Bach
      & Shakespeare to Back
         their shaky spears up)
The old Chinaman of Rich-
mond Hill who's been in his
   little brown store for God
      knows how long before we
got here & for 4 years since
& never have I seen him
unalone, with a friend,
   looking sometimes out the
window with those crazy
   red sploshes of paint
making a rail-off-effect
   3 feet from bottom, he
      has his face over there
      & is contentedly puffing his
pipe not with opium som-
      nolence but like an
         ordinary Bourgeois

tradesman at the end of day
& he's digging that dismal

little 95th St with its
 fewtrees & the redbrick
side of the bar & the few
dull lamp homes where in
the evening old walkers of
dogs mop up the last TV
news bdcast with a cup
of tea — The bare bulb
 that hangs from his ceil-
ing is so bright it lights
 to the other side of 55th
St on a dark night —
you see the red paneglass
wainscot, the washed
 strokes of red Spush
 — then the little

alarm clock on the back
 shelf — bundles of
finished shirts in shelves —

 I'm <u>bored</u>

 — the gray brown
lace in the windows of TV
parlors & he sees the sha-
dows therein of a race of

nabors he does not speak
  with — at night you
    sense his presence anyway
    in the brown backroom,
    a solitary white China
    teapot on a shelf —
        The sadness & brown
    loss of his sonless
        daughterless &

exile from Fellaheen
  days indicated by the
little narrow mirror to
the right which has a
  Joshua Reynolds <u>Blue</u> <u>Boy</u>
in its upper half panel,
now faded into a greener
  blue of mouldy time,
    & the mirror surface
    itself impossibly smokied
    by ghosts of time — the
    poor sad calendar
    finally, with month
    flap under a great
      golden breasted woman
    with gold velvet
        low cut gown — I

see the piles of white
laundry bags on floor,
the sad slant boards,
the counter — & the
huge guillotine like shadow
thrown by the parcel wrapper
& string-feeder gadget
   5 feet (much higher than
     Won Ming) high, casting
     on the wall from the
     Frisco forlorn bulb a
      monstrous China shadow
     & prophecy of more
      patience, more fires —
       somewhere brown opium
       lurks — & nightcapped
       death

But he goes on year after
year, alone, never nods
when you nod, looking out
   on the street, interior
with his own Asia of
     thots — His little
    eyes in the wrinkled worry
    of his pone Yonkers
     Mongoil bone, broz

—his thots in the back
secret does-he-live-
there room & how he
whops his lil brown
pecker, all for
future spec—

ALLEY GASTANK JAMAICA

There's a place in
Jamaica where I walked
for several months while
I was there in my last
months, north to the gas
tank,—a side alley there
ran between brokendown
fences, puddingsoft &
dark with mud holes, pits,
wrecks along the way,
the dank ramp under the
LIRR track up, parked
trucks with wood rails,
darkness of hidden thieves
like the backalleys of
Thieves Market Mexico
but no lettuce &

jungle rainslime on the ground,
   just dry American Long Is-
      land & the threat of
      150th St Negroes maybe
      hiding gone mad with the
      tiger bottle or Italian
   junk stealers hiding with
         stolen cases of grapes—
The giant tank to the
wow bloody upnight black
left with as you pass the
cemetery on the other side of
it lights down a shroud
   of spotlights so you see
sad hair grass, shroud of
   light, hunk bulk hugetank,
      gravestones of Hallowed Ghosts

—you see the little
row Colonial houses re-
done & with new quarantine
signs in the street & the
shadows in a golden
windowshade of inkblack
shack across the smooth
   newblock garage & dark
soft nights a tappin

            along to my borey
        death
            dear
                God
            please make
            me a
            writer
                again

<u>DECEMBER 1953</u>

The dead man's lips are
 pressed tasting death
 as bitter as dry musk

        ———
Soft yards of old houses
 are not for travellers
 of the late afternoon sun
 & long shadow on the ground,
 and women of 35
 with soft used thighs
 & dust motes in the
 old bed room
  Time & Sea
  Philosophy

This quality of late afternoon
in the blonde hair of mothers
in sad new parks is as
   the taste of Springtime
   in the violently parturiating
   Mind—

so make no more leaky
vows

The poisonous mushroom
is malignant because
it is inside itself, the
sac, & does not derive
   from the earth, but
   fungitates in itself,
   like a corrupt &
   unhappy man; the
   edible mushroom stems
   directly from the earth,
is in contact with it,
like a happy open
man free of cupped-in
   malignancies.
      In all writing, creative
or reflective, there's got
   to be only one way

—that is, the immediate,
the free flowing, unplanned
way. For all is pure;
the word is pure; the mind
is pure; the world is pure.
In the beginning & amen.

Because the word is
sacred it cannot be
changed.

The same as in
Doctor Sax as in the
reflection on the water.
The water does not
hesitate; the mind can
know no mud, but
what is clear in

heretofore unknown words
& word sounds ored up
from the Conscious of
the Race. But when
the words are clear, &
everything is clear, then
the other minds see
clear to think it
clear; but when the
clear words are un
clear to the other

minds, they are clear
in themselves, as is
the reflection on the
water.
     Amen.

  The words are clear as
in the reflection of
  the world on the water.
  Therefore write the
Word at once, everywhere,
from now till your
  hand is paralyzed,
for <u>there</u> will be your
work for God, since
you can not work
for God in other ways,
and would not, & dont
know how, or bend that
way, from habit, & from
  talent in the use &
    signification & arrange-
    ment of the Word.

The elephant receives
  the arrows of ill-
  natured war; you
  receive the arrows of

your genius, & work
your hand in the
    land beneath the
    skies till it cramps
    & pains thee, for
that is yr dutiful
    destiny.
        The last love allowed
    you & the least forgiv-
    able of yr final
        passions, Vain.
        Cast out the
    devils, & be pure,

— add no lines to the
finished line. Draw
no horizons beyond &
underneath the real
horizon. Blat in yr
brain the bleet sheep
bone — falsify not
the cluckings, the
    cluck-tures, in yr.
    drooly brain, brain
    child & Babe of
        Sweat & Folly. This
        your final body, final
        shame, last vanity,

greatest indulgence,
greatest farmiture,
& boon to Man,
kind literature.

SELF
by
FOOL

be the name of yr
lifework
And forget thyself
to tell the word of
the world

"Watch yr. thoughts!"

False humbleness, false
self-depreciation, leads
to useless explanation.

At the end of a
meaning is a tangent
of brain noises,
avoid them &
finish where you
finish

The brain noises belong
only in the paragraph
  of brain noises

    Canuck, dont pile
    up reasons for yr
      activities

    IN VAIN

The stars in the sky
In vain
The tragedy of Hamlet
    In vain
The key in the lock
        In vain
The sleeping mother
        In vain
The lamp in the corner
          In vain
The lamp in the corner unlit
          In vain
Abraham Lincoln
                    In vain
The Aztec empire
                      In vain
  The writing hand: in vain

(The shoetrees in the shoes
        In vain
The windowshade string upon
        the hand bible
    In vain —
    The glitter of the greenglass
        ashtray
  In vain
  The bear in the woods
        In vain
The Life of Buddha
        In vain)

FIRST OF THE NEW SKETCHES

  2 ineffectual old men
standing in the wilderness
they created but not by
their own hand, their inno-
cence & stupidity rather, &
  all the Devil had to do
    was the rest — Both in
    hats, topcoats, infinitesimal
    differences of brown hat
    vs. gray hat (felt, the
    mold of custom), pale
    blue vs. dark blue coat,

both hands apockets in
the same lost way — pants
of 2 shades shading same
size & color shanks
(white stick variety,

as befits old men se-
dentary & corrupt with
property, fear of death
& arrogant sons) — The
wilderness of their making
is the children's park
with gigantic knee-abrasing
concrete, concrete benches,
brick double shithouse
for boys' & girls' different
shameful peepees, &
over the sooty brown football
field Atlantic Ave
with its blank vehicular
passers & the huge LIRR
carshop yards with
a dozen Diesels
throbbing & exhaling bad
gas in the gray chill
December afternoon,
all around the bleak
deserted rooftops of suburban

homes, bare trees with
  boles & half dead because
hemmed at base by
concrete groundworks —
  the old men earnestly
  discuss some ineffectual
    absurdity, pointing, taking
    turns, both have glasses
    because they were taught
    to be myopic — good
  old fellows nevertheless
    as harmless as children

(children throw rocks at
              beggars)
only more culpable & a
  shade less intelligent — discussing
    eagerfaced in their
      concrete horror & scraggle
      of iron machines & air-
        stinks some unimpor-
      tant sub problem among
        the problems of the
        Problem of the West
— neckties, collars,
stamping their bloodless
  feet now & ready to
  go back in the hot

parlor to paper &
            TV

—glancing at wrist
  watches, waiting for
  gut fattening shame-
  obesity-making supper
—slaves of the bleak
  without hope
  without actual earnestness
  but momentary profitable
  appearance of so—
  contemptuous of the
  older fool is the old
  fool—Their double
  chinned cigaret smoking
  women call the chil-
  dren to home thru the
  prison of iron fences
—The older man holds
to his point, he'll soon
be mush to a new
monument in Long Island
  City Cemetery—his
hat is battereder than
  the younger oldster's,
  his mouth more twisted
pathetically—too late

now he knows he's
  got his last body —
    "Paragon" is written
on the oil truck deliv-
ering fuel to useless
furnaces — Clouds of
  soot rise from an
    old locomotive

in the yard, harking
to memories of old
  America as the Diesel
  gives 4 blasts — The
    2 old men part, one
    homeward, the other
    toiletward, hobbling,
    lost, tired, hopeless,
    looking linefaced &
  worried around the gray
  park for nothing or
  for a temporary un-
  important direction —
the sight of them reminds
me of the white light in
  the shiny wax of the
  corridor of the hosp. morgue

To drive out Angry Thoughts

Whatever anyone does,
anyone says, in the
past, now, everything, let
it bounce off the rock
  of yr gladness (yr mirror)

  Guys talking you down
  about girls
  Novelists publishing big
Towns & Cities
  Writers saying nothing
about your new writings
  Really let it bounce off
the rock of yr gladness,
  because you are
  innocent

(Free)
  Let it bounce off the
rock of your gladness the
cold, rub your hands,
drink hot brews of coffee
tea or herb, rush to yr
notebook of MEMORY BABE
  with every Memory Tic

CHURCH MUSIC—
  Organ clamoring
with the rising chorus,
  the holy voices of
  oo-lips of littleboys
  in white lace collars,
    the overvault gloom
        OO huge

        SATURDAY   dec. 12
      ETERNITY BOYS

    The tall sexual Negro
boy on the junkyard
street near the Gas
  Tank Jamaica, about 7
or 8 yrs old, he was
running his palm along
  his fly in some Sexual
story to the other little
boy Negro who had his
arm around him as they
came up the street in
the gray rain of Satur-
day afternoon—smoke
  emanating from junk fires,
    smell of burnt rubber, piles

of tires, junk shops
   with old white stoves
on the blackmud sidewalk,
rusty clinkered grates,
   black mudholes, the pudding
   soft rained-on tar. the
   boards with rot in em &
old nails, piles of plaster
   & lath, dirty neons of
   late afternoon bars beyond
   the wet sag of the
   woodfence — the thrill
      & mist & hugeness of
      it & all on Saturday,
   the 2 boys have been
   arm in arm buddying
all day in this wilderness
      of their souls & now
         the tall one to the

littler kid his personality
so huge, hobloo-gooboo
   African, vast, is demons-
   trating that boy-sex &
   they are grave discussing it
   — as I come along I
see but pretend not to
& they peek to see if

old Walt Whitman see
but old Walt Whitman's
in a ragged secret coat,
  holding down all his lids
  & not Whitmaned—
inconspicuous—I thought
  "How infinitely Huge
is the tall one's personality
  & the Epic of their

Graymist Saturday today
  as Jamaica Ave. swarms
with Xmas shoppers, the
sad Americans with childrens
  & families spending all their
money, the phoney Xmas
  Santas & cups & tinsel
storewindows—These 2
  black angels of Raggedy
Saturday Real demon-
strating in their freedom
  boyhood how great arts
  like bop are born,
  arm-in-arm & interested
  in nothing but themselves,
    lovers and pure as they'll
    never be again—
  in the backlot too

they play with their
cocks & show the shiver
   & itchpain to the rain
& rub the rotwood &
   try to come, the shuddering
out-to-the-world push of
loins, & wonder — but
   in the face the inescapable
   & eternal Personality
   (the tall one a cloth
cap, the littler a
   wooldown) vastness
of nose, cheek, informa-
   tive push tout be
      dra man talisman
         eyes of the

   King of all the gangs
& possible Prophets of
   the world, Littler is so
amazed & what he could
   tell you this minute about
   Tall would fill 17 <u>Visions</u>
   <u>of Codys</u>   8500000
      pages of tight prose
         if he could only talk
      & tell it, in the shack
what he done yesterday,

       the madness of his
     secret humor, fact,
     let Littler talk": -
         "Why he in the
         bed mattress is the

     long black funny boy
     Sam I seen him
     tho a rock clear
     thu the smoke &
       had sixteen harmonicas
   in his eyes & in his
   eyes I seen Sixteen
     signs & he says 'Boy,
       dear Lord, I'm seen
       the ghost agin last
   night & Paw come
       home & Howdie Doodie
         Television Show &
         Silvercup Bread & My
         Sister bought it &
         <u>smile</u>" — however

   one can do it, it is
   the Enormousness of
   the Universe that makes
   the Microcosm its tiniest

unit even Enormous-er,
— so 2 little Negro
boys arm in arm on
  Saturday rainy after-
  noon contain in them-
  selves the history of
mankind if they could
but talk & tell it
  all about themselves
  & what they done &
  if an observer could
  follow them around

& see & judge the
vastness of every tiny
unit — Who knows
the vast religiousness
of that cloth cap
when it shines radiant
in the mind of the
  littler boy, or when
  grown up & 's forgot
  Sam & gone 3,000
  miles to nothing the sudden
memory of Great Sam
(MY BOYHOOD PAL)
    will be as remembering

the Angel of Heaven &
      All Hope,
    since dying

       *   *   *

GIRL IN LUNCHCART

Girl in front of me
with green sweater red
  lips gentle thin cold
  fingers at her hair &
  she's explaining (at her
    high stiff hair like hairdos
of Africa) explaining to
  girlfriend whose smile I
  see reflected in shiny
  mirror back of Jamaica
  Ave. Lunchcart Cash
    Register — 5 P M of
an October afternoon, the
young counterman unshaved
  goodlooking hangs around
swaying & half smiling
pretending to work with
  checks at that booth —

Tired puff eyed Greek
oldworker who spends
Sat nites in Turkish
baths of NY

voyeuring Americans &
  heroboy queers of
Lower 2nd Avenue comes in
for big exciting afterwork
meal of Chicken Croquettes
with Sauce & will be
  here T'Giving day for big
  Turkey with works —
  sad to live, quick to
  eat, early to work,
  slow to sleep, long to
  die — Now so the
  girl uncaring of old men
& pain has her fore finger
against her temple
  while listening to other girl
  speak & therefore in
  nodding seriousness has
  ravelled all her eyebone
  skin up in a mask
  of ark ugly furrow

destiny having no relation
to the hazel glitter,
  the nutty mystery of
  her sweet eyes & suckkiss
  lips & long drawndown
    <u>bosh</u> <u>flop</u> face discon-
  torted by further arrangements
  of leanface on palm—
  in her delicate edible
  ear a dull metal thing—
    her lips fully lipsticked
    & curved like Cupid &
      stain the coffee cup—
      her eye on her girlfriend
        cold, watchful, secretive,
      pretending to be curious,
      like she'll make the
      parody-story of this
        gossip tonight in
        earwigging dreams in
          her fragrant thigh
              sheets! whee

LATE AUTUMN afternoon,
the birds are whistle-singing zeet
feor in the dry tinder twig trees,
  they 'fleet' & in the general
  traffic ("Spr-r-e e e t")

rush on Atlantic Ave. & the double
go ahead Diesel BOT - BOT in
the LIRR yards they wait
between calls as if, in the
activity of their own afternoon,
they had intervals too, time too
& orders from the parchesi chess
board to air conditioner machines
of the Glum Window World
make their little fluttery wait
wake, leaves falling not even
with you could hear the <u>tick</u>
of their little fall on the concrete
ground beneath which Indians
lie ancestral bone by skull in

tomahawk New York —
the fishtail back end of
some new car parked beyond
the Eternity Porch (like the
one in San Jose where I was
so high at gray dawn I heard
between the vibrating yowls of
Neal's baby the great rush
of wave sounds wave on wave
shuddering & Vibrating like one
vast electric or bio electric
or cosmic gravity "struay

ill" — —z o o n g g—
scared me & made me hear
the moment moth sound of
Time, good or bad old Time
I'm in, and'll write
for — So now to
"INDIANS
IN THE
RAILROAD
EARTH")

— late afternoon Autumn in
Long Island, the leaf slants
down in the wind & hits the
ground & bounces & goes 'chuck'
— as dry as that — the others
already fallen lie heaped in
chlorophyll green grass between
  driveway concretes — the
  sky has a rose tint in its
  gray demeanor — the leaves/rose brown yellow
    transparent/& like drunken poets emptying/
    uselessness in pages
  Never did try to get
on a car via standing
on a journal box except
one time on a splintery

flatcar & even then
I was as helpless as
a baby, one slack
 bang pop I'd have
 been as helpless as
 a bread bun rolling
 off to get run over
  & flattened in the
 middle & be toast
  by Fall— — —

SAN FRANCISCO SKETCH (1954 now)

America's truck and car kick has
made it place twin radio antennas
on the last hill of hope overlooking
 the Pacific to the Orient Sea.
 Clouds of sorrow pass over and
into a nameless blue opening beyond
 the storms of San Francisco. Lonely
men with open collars and gray
 fedoras take long drear street
 walks where oil trucks turn into
  gray garage doorways at 2:30
  Sunday afternoon. Wash hopelessly
flaps on the roofs of Skid Row
where the great Proletariat has

come to stake his claim, or
claim his stake, one.

Everything is taking place inside
dark windows that have the
quality of inky pools inside which
white fish are swimming motionlessly
across extended arm rests, now
and then peeking out to take a
quick look at the street, flapping
  grayed muslin curtains back to
  shield the furtive sorrow. Rain
    spats across the scene in a sudden
    shower from the tormented sky
all radiant with sun holes and
Frisco Gray and Black rain
clouds radiating from the sea
like a vast slow unfolding of
its rainy tragedy where driving
rains smash futilely on the
blank waving void.
                    Hopeless blue
boxes intended for plants or
  for the outdoor coolness of
  Spreckels' Homo Milk and
  8¢ cubes of Holiday Oleo-
margarine, stick out from

windowsills in and around what
the City Managers call the "blighted

area" that must be torn down
within 5, or even 3, years. Dis-
possession and complete loneliness
haunt the empty sidewalks in
front of old stores for rent.
In a tenement a little Negro
girl in dumb thought at her
mother's sofa alone in the
afternoon room reads "Hardened
vegetable oils (soybean & cottonseed),
skim milk, salt, monoglyceride,
lecithin; isopropyl citrate (0–01%)
to protect flavor, and vitamin
A and artificial color added.
2 oz. supplies 47% of adults
and 62% of child's minimum
daily Vitamin A requirements,"
from the cube of oleo paper
and stares for 90 seconds in a
Buddhist-like trance at the
little ®(apparently meaning
'registered' trademark) at the
side of the brand name
Holiday, wondering if the

little ⓡ is meant to be a
secret of the recipe not mentioned
in the long paragraph, or a
sign of some authority hidden
behind the butter in a suit and
briefcase with Ⓢ on it and
ⓡ on his Cadillac and he
drives around with bulging eyes
and a Texas Truman hat in
the streets of the City.

"I, poor French Canadian Ti Jean become
a big sophisticated hipster esthete in
the homosexual arts, I, mutterer to
myself in childhood French, I, Indian-
head, I, Mogloo, I the wild one,
the "wild boy," I, Claudius Brutus
McGonigle Mckarroquack, hopper
of freights, Skid Row habituee,
railroad Buddhist, New England Modernist,
20th Century Storywriter, Crum, Krap,
dope, divorcee, hype, type; sitter in win-
dows of life; idiot far from home; no
wood in my stove, no potatoes in my

field, no field; hepcat, howler, wailer,
waiter in the line of time; lazy
washed-out, workless; yearner after
  Europe, poet manquée; <u>pas</u> <u>tough!</u>

stool gatherer, food destroyer, war
evader, nightmare dreamer, angel
be-er, wisdom seer, fool, bird, cocacola
bottle — I, am in need of advice
from God and will not get it, not
  likely, nor soon, nor ever — sad saha
  world, we were born for nothing from
  nothing — Respects to our sensitive
    Keeners up & down the crime."

O Melville! thy Soul
  Sustains me
  More than all the Buddhas
That have passed
With the water
Under the Brooklyn Bridge

                        * * *

NY

Dont let your New York be modified &
shrunken by local transitory dislikes (such
as Tony Bennett-Laurels-bleak N.Y.) (in
all this Applish Apple) — but the Liberté
  steaming in in brightgold afternoon, of
  the Daily News, 4 AM bars, Birdland,
  Jackie Gleason, Italian restaurants,
  5th Avenue, Lucien, Wolfe, Charley
Vackner the race results, West St. water-
front, Friday night fights in the TV saloon,
the Columbia Campus in May, the Remo, hep-
  cats on corners bent, Pastrami at the Gaiety,
an ice cream soda at midnight on Broadway,
  beautiful gorgeous blondes, brunettes, —
        But I hate the fumes of 34th St.
  A strange aura of ma-
sochism and even of homo-
sexuality in Christian Cathol-
icism — "He will give you a
  taste of joys & delights that
transcend anything" — etc —
. . . That's the homosexuality . . .
"praying to God to rid you of
  your desires and <u>abase</u> you thus"
the masochism —
    Why?

You cant beat the Tao —
the Buddha — the Guru of
the Far East — "and Jesus
will make it <u>easy</u>" — <u>Really
my dear</u> — <u>Nothin's easy</u>.

The difference between Merton
and me, is, I didnt fall
for the columbia jester

TANGIERS 1957

Blowing in an afternoon wind,
on a white fence,
A cobweb

March wind from the sea — a lonely dobe house
with red tiled roof, on a highway boulevard,
by white garages and new apartment buildings
in ruined field — everything in place in the in-
scrutable sunny air, no meaning in the sky and
a girl running by coughing! It is very strange how
the green hills are full of trees and white houses
without comment. I think Tangiers is some kind
of city. Man and son cross road, wearing
green Sabbath fez caps, like papercup cakes
good nuf to eat — I think I'm sposed to be

alive—I dont see anything around—Drops
of whitewash on this red concrete plaza with
the whitewashed tower by the sea for
Muezzins of the Sherifian Star—The
other night, here, Arab bagpipes—

Spring is coming—
Yep, all that equipment
For sighs

ZOCO CHICO — TANGIERS —

a weird Sunday in Fellaheen
Arabland with you'd expect
mystery white windows &
do see but b God the broad
up there in whiten
my-veil is sitting & peering
by a Red Cross, above a lil
sign says PRACTICANTES
Servicio Permanente
TF NO. ✚ 9766
the cross being red—this
is over a tobacco shop
with luggage & pictures,
a little barelegged boy
leaning on counter with a

family of wristwatched
  Spaniards — Limey sailors
  from the submarines pass
  trying to get drunker & drunker
  yet quiet & lost in home
  regret & two little Arab
  hepcats have a brief musical
    confab (boys of 10) & they
  part with a push of arms
& wheeling of arms, the cat
  has a yellow skullcap &
  a blue zoot suit

  I am now hi on
    MAHOUN
  M A H O U N
Cakes of kief boiled with
  spices & candies —
eaten with hot tea —
the black & white tiles
of the outdoor cafe
  are soiled by lonely
Tangiers time — A
little bald cropped
boy walks by, goes
  to men at table,
  says "Yo!" then
  the waiter throws

him out, "Yig" —
    A brown ragged robe
priest sits with me at
table, but looks
    off with hands
      on lap at brilliant
        red fez & red girl
      sweater & red boy
      shirt green scene

RAILROAD BUFFET IN AVIGNON

    A priest who looks exactly
like Bing Crosby but with a long gray beard,
chewing bread, then rushes out, with beret and
briefcase. . . . .

PARIS SIDEWALK CAFE

                Now, on sidewalk in
sun, the racket of going-to-work same as
in Houston or in Boston and no better —
But it is a vast promise I feel here, endless
streets, stores, girls, places, meanings, I can
see why Americans stay here — <u>First
man in Paris I looked at was a dignified</u>

<u>Negro gentleman in a homburg</u>—The human
types are endless, old French ladies, Malayan
girls, schoolboys, blond student boys, tall
young brunettes, hippy pimply secretaries,
beret'd goggled clerks, beret'd scarved
earners of milk bottles, dikes in long blue
laboratory coats, frowning older students striding
in trench coats like Boston, seedy little
rummy cops fishing thru their pockets (in
blue caps), cute pony tailed blondes in high
heels with zip notebooks, goggled bicyclists
with motors attached, bespectacled homburgs
walking reading Le Parisien, bushy headed
mulattos with long cigarettes in mouth,

old ladies carrying milkcans & shopping bags,
rummy WCFieldses spitting in the gutter hands
a pockets going to their printing shop for
another day, a young Chinese looking French
girl of 12 with separated teeth looking
Like she's in tears (frowning, & with a bruise
on her shin, schoolbooks in hand, cute and
serious like Mardou), porkpie executive
running and catching bus sensationally
vanishing with it, mustached long haired
Italian youths, regular types coming in
the bar for their morning shot of wine,
huge bumbling bankers in expensive suits

fishing for newspaper pennies in their
palms (bumping into women at the bus
stop), piped jews with packages, a
lovely redhead with dark glasses pip pip
pip on her heels trots to work bus, a
waitress slopping mop water in the old old
gutter, ravishing brunettes with tightfitting
skirts succeeding in making you want to
grab their rounded ass (tho they dont deign
to look), goofely plup plup schoolgirlies
with long boyish bobs plirping lips over
books & memorizing lessons fidgetly, lovely
young girls of 17 on corners who walk
off with low-heeled sure-strides in long
red coats to downtown Paris smokepot
    Old Napoleon wonders—leading a dog,
an apparent East Indian, whistling, with
books—bearded bus riders riding to
accounting school—dark similar-lipped
serious young lovers, boy arming girlshoulders
—statue of Danton pointing nowhere—

—Paris hepcat in dark glasses waiting there,
faintly mustached—little suited boy in
black beret, with well off father—English
    Flag waving, red and white crisscrossing on
a blue field—(for Queen's visit)

PARIS PARK

Sitting in a little park in Place Paul Painlevé
—a curving row of beautiful rosy tulips rigid
and swaying, fat shaggy sparrows, beautiful
  shorthaired mademoiselles (one shd. never be
  alone at night in Paris, boy or girl, but I'm
an evil old man & world hater who will
become the greatest writer who ever lived)

RESTING BY A WINDOW IN THE LOUVRES

—Seine outside, Carrousel Bridge, gray
rain clouds, pushing overhead, blue sky
holes, Seine ripple silver, old dark
  stone & houses, distant domes, skeletal
  Eiffel, people on sidewalks like Guardini's
little brushstroke people — (with black
dot heads)—In this Vast hall where I
sit, more'n 600 feet long, with dream
giant canvases everywhere, the murmur
blur of hundreds of voices—Seine waters
restlessly greening near the bridge, trees
blooming, tomorrow London—

*   *   *   *   *   *

Downtown London Spring 1957 (sketch) —
hammering of iron, banging of planks, a
drill, rrrttt, humbuzz of traffic, morble
of voices, peet of bird, dling of wrench
  falling on pavement (or of bolt screwer),
  truck going brruawp, squeak of brakes,
  the impersonal bangbang & beep beep
  of London still building long after
  Shakespeare & Blake lie bedded in
  stone & sheep — April in London,
    Where is Gray?

TRAIN TO SOUTHAMPTON

Brain trees growing out of Shakespeare's fields
— dreaming meadows full of lamb-dots —
The dreary town of St. Denys, a church with a
pasted-on concrete arch on the roof, the
crowded row of redbrick houses, old man in
a garden blossoming a new English Spring
which seems to me hope-devoid. . . . .

SOUTHHAMPTON — ridiculous little boxcars in the
yards . . . cranes in the haze . . . cyclists . . .
little boy sitting a wall horse style, with boots
  . . . fweet of our engine —

————

BACK TO AMERICA AND MEXICO
SKETCH SATURDAY MEXICO 1957

For a long time I didnt notice that
  a big dog was laying in the grass
  six feet behind me, completely
  licenseless, no collar, naked &
  glad the true dog sleeps, when
  I call him he pays no attention,
  right in the middle of the city
  park he stretches & enjoys —
Meanwhile 2 little girls play
  with a ball (too small to throw
  it) as the mother waits patiently
  standing with shopping bag — 2
  boys kick the soccer ball &
then quit, one falls flat on
  his back in the grass arms out-
  spread to the sky while the other
  dances little steps & sings —
    An ordinary man carrying an
empty pail — Two guys pulling
a roll truck with one tire on
  it, talking — A little boy
  comes by playing with a

                plastic bottle tied around
                    his neck with straps—
        Gangs of little children
        rush up to push the park-
        worker's lawnmower with
        him, he grins—A dark
        Mexican kid with handfulstring
            of huge balloons blowing
            his little air tweeter—
            The dog is up, near the
        ball boys, watching nobly—
        he hops on 3 legs, his right
            front foot is broken or hurt,
            now he hops up to see a
            ragged boy's white dog on
                rope leash & a short fight
                breaks out—The little boy
                brings his dog over to tell me
                the whole story (in Spanish)
                of his wounds & bravery—
                The ordinary man returns with
                    full pail, hobbling—The mother
                & little girls, sit now on the
                    old iron cannon, she reads
                    as they crawl gladly—(I'm not
            interested much in sex anymore, but
        in that mother smiling patiently while
            the little girls play)

SKETCH OF BEGGAR

The strange Allen Ansen-looking
but fat chubby Mexican beggar standing
in front of Woolworth's on Coahuila
behaving spastically, with short haircut
of bangs, brown suitcoat, white shirt,
big pot belly, rocking back & forth
jiggling his hand (left or right, as / according
to which other he rests in his pocket)
& he really makes it, / I just saw 3 people give him
money in one minute, as one
charitied him he turned away &
scratched his brow (murmured some-
thing?)—He cant conceive that
someone (as I) can be watching from
  across the street 2nd story window
  & so I see all his in-between
    actions & attitudes, a definite
  (holy) phoney, (I mean his
  life is harder than mine by far),
  when it came time for him to
  blow his nose after sneezing
  he didnt shake spastically
  but efficiently withdrew a
napkin from his coat & blew
  his nose <u>hard</u> 3 times then
  put it back in his pocket
—

—Even poor women give him
   coins & he places all of them
 in a funny space behind his back
 belt—His feet are tired, he
   whomps them up in a dance &
                down—

When fat businessman glides
by blowing smoke contemptly
at him he hangs his head in
contemplative shame—He
   looks up, scratches his neck,
   feels his coat pocket, sways,
   & waits beneath the light
               (as I)
   (Who've just finished a T-bone
                       steak
                          in Kuku's)

     Above him I see dim
figures in the Woolworth
   storerooms as of dance-
   class-ing & mamboing
              —

Being as I am now off drugs,
after a fine meal I feel like
I did as a kid in Lowell, an
   excited happy mind—It's

Saturday in Mex City & the streets
   lead to all kinds of fascinating
   lighted vistas, movies, stores, pepsi
   colas, whorehouses, nightclubs,
   children playing in brownstreet
   lamps & the sleep of the
   Fellaheen dog in some old
   grand doorway

YES, the end to a perfect meal
   is always the grand cup of
   black coffee, here or in
Sweets Seafood Restaurant, NY
or in Paree, anywhere, the
warm rich comforter (which
prepares the appetite for chocolates
 on the homeward walk, preferably
milk chocolate & nuts) —
   It's the exciting hour in MCity
or anycity, 8 on Sat nite, when
the 5 & 10's closing & the show
 crowds rush & newsboys shout,
   trolley bells clang, like soft
   like Lowell long ago when
   I had that swarming vision

FINIS

Jack Kerouac
BOOK OF SKETCHES

PENGUIN POETS